7 June 2001

HARRY McCREEDY

for Timothy

Please take
this work "from the
heart" into your
own heart and
learn its lessons
well —

Friends
always,

Jeff

HARRY McCREEDY

A NOVEL

JAMES JEFFREY PAUL

ELDERBERRY PRESS

ELDERBERRY PRESS
1393 Old Homestead Road, Second Floor
Oakland, Oregon 97462—9506
elderberrypress@usa.net
TEL/FAX:541.459.6043

Publisher's Catalog-in-Publication Data
Harry McCreedy/James Jeffrey Paul
ISBN: 1-930859-04-X

1. Race Relations.
2. Affirmative Action.
3. Politics
4. Business
5. Fiction
I. Title

This book was written, printed, and bound
in the United States of America

. This book is dedicated with love to my two dearest friends

MICHELE ANNETTE GARIBALDI

and

MARNIE ADELE ALLEN

for all the joy that knowing them has been

CHAPTER ONE

In our time, violence in the workplace has become so common that only a spectacular example of it can command the public's attention. For this reason, the tragedy at the Pennsylvania Avenue branch of the Port Arthur Shoe Company in downtown Washington, D.C., which took the lives of an assistant sales manager and his new bride, went virtually unnoticed. A creative reporter with dreams of glory tried to play up the event, which he labeled "the Port Arthur Shoes Massacre," but his editor immediately crushed those dreams. "You can't call something in which only two people were killed a massacre!" the editor declared as he cut the reporter's story mercilessly and consigned it to an inside page.

Police reports insist that the "massacre" took place on the day after Labor Day, on Tuesday, the fifth of September in the year 2000, but the origins of the event (to the extent that any event can be said to have a single origin) began just under a year before, on Monday, the thirteenth of September, 1999, when the new assistant sales manager arrived at the Pennsylvania Avenue branch of Port Arthur Shoes for his first day on the job.

Harold Michael McCreedy was twenty-two years old and neither one thing nor the other. Looking at his long, thin features, his pale skin and high forehead, his thin lips and soft hands with ridiculously long fingers, his short, neatly-combed pale brown hair and china blue eyes that (although he had perfect vision) looked out somewhat myopically at the world, one might have tagged him a meek intellectual. When one considered the clothes he wore on this particular morning—an old-fashioned English double-breasted suit with matching vest, red silk tie, wing-tipped shoes, and pocket watch on a fob—one might have gone farther and branded him as one of those intelligent but ineffectual people who find meaning and a sense of identity in adopting the styles of past eras. But to do so would have been to ignore the slightly rakish way in which Harry's clothes hung on his body, the latent power that lurked coiled within him, and how imposing was the sheer bulk of his six-foot-one-inch, one-hundred-and-seventy-pound frame. A keen and perceptive intelligence shone in the depths of his timid eyes; his delicate hands moved with a languid grace that implied an overwhelming, barely repressed sensuality.

Harry could hardly believe that he was about to undertake this job in the business world, and his surviving relatives could not believe it at all. Harry had always been the weakling of the family, a genetic accident in an otherwise robust, thriving gene pool. His father's family, the McCreedys, had a long, proud history of achievement in business, science, and the priesthood, both in the British Isles and (since long before the Revolution) in America. They saw themselves as fierce warriors in an endless struggle for their Faith and their family honor, and against the world. Harry, although his piety and academic achievements were as great as, if not greater than, any of the McCreedys , had never displayed much acumen for dealing with the world, or any drive to succeed; he seemed destined to end his days the way he had initially planned—as a professor of history or the classics. It was true that other McCreedys had attained great reputations in academia, but Harry seemed too weak-willed to achieve greatness even in that sanctuary for the timid.

All of this might have been forgivable, but for the accident of Harry's parentage. His father, David, had been the shining star of his generation of the family, a much-decorated bomber pilot in the Vietnam War, an honors graduate of Harvard Business School, and a superb manager of several of the family businesses. His sudden death of a heart attack in June of 1987 had been a devastating blow to the family, one from which it never fully recovered. To compound the loss, David left behind a sorry pair of survivors: his crazy wife Elizabeth and their weakling son, ten-year-old Harry.

The McCreedys had never liked Elizabeth; she was too bohemian with her ornate shawls, beads, and wildly colored dresses, her passion for embroidery and painting surrealistic watercolors. Despite her strong religious faith and the fact that her husband and son adored her, there was something unfocused about her, something impractical and ethereal. To make matters worse, she suffered from periodic depressions, and while her son Harry seemed free of this defect, it was clear that his overall weakness of character resulted from his mother's defective genes.

Soon after her husband died, Elizabeth suffered a breakdown so severe that she had to be hospitalized, and the doctors said they had no idea when, if ever, she would recover. So Harry was thrust upon the mercy of his father's family—his mother was an orphan with no living relatives. His father had left enough money in his will to pay for Harry's education up to and including college, so the McCreedys were spared the odious task of spending a great deal of their own money on this unworthy person. They did, however, have to provide him with room and board, a task that they accepted, albeit reluctantly, for family honor forbade simply casting Harry adrift. Over the next eight years, until he went away to college, Harry stayed with many family members, but never in one place for long, because no one could tolerate him. Some family members were nicer to him than others—his grandfather, for instance, treated him in a distant and stern manner, but did not abominate him altogether, while his Aunt Susan would scream insults at him and pummel him with her fists. But he endured, thanks to his faith and his unshakable conviction that one day his mother would be released from the hospital, and they would be reunited.

Elizabeth's breakdown proved to be so severe that, for a year, she could not communicate with anyone. Then her cognitive powers returned, and finally she could talk with her son, her only visitor, in a manner reasonably similar to the old times. She did not have much opportunity to do so, however, for her late husband's family tried its best to keep Harry away from her. It was not until Harry was in college that he had the freedom to visit her as often as he liked. It was at that same time that her doctors pronounced her able to reenter the world; she could have improved sooner had she received decent medical care, but her husband's family would not spend a penny on her, and she had been forced to depend upon the inferior care of a charity hospital in the suburbs of Washington, D.C. Harry vowed, however, that he would get his mother out of the hospital as soon as he graduated and got a job.

It was around the time of his mother's half-hearted recovery that Harry, suddenly and with little thought or prayer on his part, made a momentous decision. He had been majoring in history and the classics; now he changed his major to one of the family's specialties, business. When his grandfather heard of this, he ordered Harry to come to the family estate for a talk.

"Why are you doing this, Harry?" the old man demanded sternly.

"I want to prove myself, grandfather," the young man replied hesitantly, but with an essential composure that startled him. "I want to do what the family does. I want to be a part of it."

"The desire to do something for which you have no aptitude is a foolish waste," his grandfather said.

"I believe I do have an aptitude for it, sir," Harry replied, his composure beginning to give way. "Of course, I can't prove that, but—I wouldn't have chosen this path unless I felt, within myself, that I did have that aptitude somewhere, deep down."

"Delusional thinking," the old man sniffed.

"Perhaps," Harry agreed and then, overwhelmed, fell silent.

Grandfather McCreedy regarded Harry for a moment, and his hard gaze gradually softened—not with sympathy, but under the influence of some new, dawning insight. "Harry, are you doing this thinking that you'll earn more money in business, and that then you'll be able to get your mother out of the hospital?"

"Well, that would be an additional benefit, but no, sir, that's not what inspired me to do this."

A faint glimmer of astonishment shone in his grandfather's eyes. "You mean that you actually *want* to improve yourself?"

"Yes, sir."

"Extraordinary," the old man mumbled, then fell into deep thought. When he emerged he said, "Well, Harry, I'm heartened by this change of affairs. I'm not going to surrender to my enthusiasm, though, because, like the rest of the world, I judge by results, not intentions. But here is what I'll do. Your father's estate has paid for your college education, and you'll be graduating in a couple of years. After that, I was going to tell you that you were on your own, except for the five hundred dollars a month that you'll receive from the family trust. We can't stop you from receiving that pittance—much as some of us would like to, and as I wanted to, until just now. Well, you will still be on your own when you graduate, but with this possibility: If, over a space of time—and I'm not talking about a few months— you prove that you do have business ability, then we will consider letting you work with us, and might even consider letting you partake fully of the family largesse. But until then, you're on your own."

Dizzy with shock, Harry could only nod and mumble, "Yes, sir, thank you."

And now here he was, an honors graduate of a good business program, standing on a busy street in downtown Washington not far from the White House and the Capitol, with a tide of humanity surging all around him on foot and in automobiles, about to put his determination to prove himself to its first practical test. He had moved to the city (which he had always loved) two weeks ago, and had rented a small walk-up apartment in Georgetown; the money he had received thus far from his meager trust fund was enough to pay the rent on the apartment for several months in advance. Once he started earning his salary of $20,500 a year, he would be able both to pay his rent and get his mother out of the hospital. The thought of her filled him with a sense of pain and loss. The doctors had recently informed him that his mother had developed a coronary disease, which was too far advanced for them to do anything about, and she would only live for another year or so. There was no time to waste.

Harry inspected his reflection in the store's front window and was satisfied with his appearance. He crossed himself and, as he always did before embarking upon any major undertaking, said the prayer to his patron, Saint Michael the Archangel, the leader of the Heavenly Host, the one who had cast Satan down into Hell:

> Saint Michael the Archangel, defend us in battle. Be our protection against the wickedness and snares of the devil. May God rebuke him, we humbly pray; and do thou, O Prince of the Heavenly Host, by the power of God thrust into Hell Satan and all evil spirits who wander through the world seeking the ruin of souls. Amen.

Then he opened the front door and walked through it.

CHAPTER TWO

The main showroom seemed almost as large as an indoor stadium. Its length was bisected by eight main aisles, on either side of which were spaced twelve rows of display shelves. Along the walls, from the floor to the ceiling fifty feet above, were stacked thousands of boxes of shoes; wheeled ladders set into brackets on the walls afforded access to this bounty. Harry, an amateur antiquarian and hence a lover of architecture, noted with approval that the high ceiling was vaulted, and had a large skylight set into its apex.

A short, squat woman who, had she been a few inches taller, would have seemed less fat than she was, came walking up. Harry had already met her; she was Bernice Stilton, the other assistant sales manager. Her dirty brown hair, now going gray, clung to the sides and top of her head in a riot of messy curls; her plump face was largely unwrinkled, but her skin had a dull, ashy color, as though it had already begun to crumble back into dust. Bernice seldom smiled, so she greeted Harry with a nod and a handshake. "Hey, Harry," she said in her flat Midwestern drawl.

"Hello, Bernice," Harry replied. His voice, with its tones of Back Bay urbanity, suddenly seemed to echo throughout the cavernous room, and its sound took him aback. There would probably be only one other New Englander among the staff, at best; the rest would probably find his accent a novelty, or a cause for amusement. Harry was overcome with anxiety. Would they not respect him because of it? And he was probably much better educated than any of them—would they consider him a pompous prig, or envy him because of his supposed privilege? (If they only knew...)

"Nice to have you aboard," Bernice said. "Well, like I told you, this first week you won't have much to actually do. You'll just be following me around and learning the ropes. The store won't actually open for another two hours, and we won't have a sales meeting until the end of the day, so why don't you just come with me and get a cup of coffee and meet some of the people you'll be trying to manage?"

"That would be great," Harry replied. She led him down the aisles toward the back of the store. "A very nice place," he remarked. "And huge. You wouldn't feel confined working in a place like this."

Bernice snorted. "Well, sometimes the atmosphere gets a little tight around here."

"What do you mean?"

"You'll learn."

Harry felt a chill of unease. Were the people here hard to get along with? He told himself to have courage, it was only his first day.

Bernice and Harry passed through a swinging door at the back of the showroom marked EMPLOYEES ONLY and walked down a hall to the break room. Three people—a plump young black woman, a fat middle-aged man, and a skinny youth who seemed even younger than Harry—sat at the tables drinking coffee and (in the fat man's case) eating a Danish. "Want some coffee?" Bernice asked.

"Yes, please," said Harry.

"Regular or decaf?"

Harry chuckled. "Since it's my first day on the job, you'd better make it extra-strength!"

Bernice gave a little smile. "Honey, before long, electric jolts to your heart won't revive you."

Harry felt another, stronger chill of unease. What was wrong here? He must learn what it was before it harmed him.

"You want cream and sugar?" she asked.

"Yes, please, a lot of both."

Bernice prepared his coffee and handed him the cup. "Thank you," Harry said. "Can I meet the people here?"

Bernice raised her eyebrows. "You actually *want* to meet them?"

"Why…of course," Harry said, a little bewildered.

She frowned and said, "Come on." First she led Harry to the plump young black woman. She was, if not exactly attractive, at least charming-looking, with a smooth, round face, straight hair pulled back with a hair comb, and more than a hint of mischief in her dark brown eyes. Harry guessed that she was, at most, only two or three years older than he.

"Denise, this is our new assistant sales manager, Harry McCreedy," Bernice told her. "Harry, meet Denise Andrews, our best salesperson."

"Pleased to meet you, Denise," Harry said, extending his hand. The girl gripped his hand and pumped it vigorously, but the pleasant feel of her soft, plump skin offset the discomfort of her vise-like handshake. The sensation, like the woman, did not fill Harry with desire, but rather with a vague sense of comfort.

"Pleased to meet you, Harry," she said. "So you just got out of school, huh?"

"Yes, I did."

"Your first real job, huh?"

"Yes."

"Well, it'll also be your last."

"Beg pardon?"

"Honey, when you're finished with this job, you're never going to want to work again. Go on welfare, be a homeless person, anything will seem better to you than this."

"Now, Denise," Bernice chided.

"I'm just telling the boy the truth. Well, it's nice to have you aboard anyway, Harry."

"Thanks," Harry said, his unease growing.

Denise's eyes blazed with mischief. "Tell me one thing. You ain't been laid in a long time, have you?"

"Denise!" Bernice cried.

"Bernice, I'm just asking him a question. You ain't been laid in a long time, Harry, have you? That stuff has backed up all over your body and made you all uptight. You need to get laid. Then all that stuff'll be drained out of you, and you'll feel all loose and funky."

"DENISE!" Bernice yelled. "That's enough!"

"Uh—thanks for the advice," Harry muttered, blushes burning his cheeks. It was true. He had not been with a woman in a long time. His experience with sex had been minimal, anyway. How he wished that it were otherwise—and how he wished, with equal fervor, that he could follow the Church's teachings and preserve himself for marriage. Just one of many ideals that he had fallen short of. Nevertheless, for now he could not—or did not feel that he could, or did not want to—control his raging libido, or his desire to ravish every attractive woman he met, and to receive from them some vital, missing part of himself.

As Bernice hustled him over to the next table, she whispered, "I apologize for her. She's just immature for her age. She's a great salesperson, though." Then she spoke to the fat, middle-aged man. "Richard, this is our new assistant sales manager, Harry McCreedy."

Richard pulled his bulk out of his chair carefully and extended his hand. "Pleased to meet you, Harry," he said in a deep, rumbling voice. "I'm Richard Jenkins."

"Nice to meet you, Richard," Harry said.

"You know, Harry, Richard used to be a college professor," Bernice remarked. "He's very educated, like you."

"Oh, really?" Harry asked, interested and perplexed.

"Yes," Richard said. "I was a professor of ancient history at George Washington for over fifteen years. Then my marriage broke up, my wife took the kids, the house, and most of the money, and so I had nothing left to work for. I was getting sick of academia anyway, all the backbiting and the pressure and the scrambling for position, plus my department was starting to go politically correct, and it was terrible—if you didn't agree with all of those bullshit political doctrines, you were considered an outcast. It was like Stalinist Russia. So I quit, and went back to retail—I put myself through college and graduate school by working retail, you know—and then I found out that things are even worse here!" He gave a sharp laugh, amused yet bitter.

"The academic world can be a pretty awful place to work," replied Harry.

"And now, let's meet Albert, our youngest salesperson," Bernice said, leading him over to the next table. "He's a year younger than you, Harry."

"Well, nice to know I have some seniority!" Harry quipped nervously.

"Albert, this is our new assistant sales manager, Harry McCreedy," Bernice told the young man, who looked up and regarded the pair with studied indifference. He was a skinny young man with a military-style haircut and a sickly pallor to his skin. "Hello," he said in his languid, nasal voice, and did not extend his hand.

"Nice to meet you, Albert—what's your full name?"

"McKenzie," the youth replied. "Albert McKenzie."

"Oh!" Harry said. "A good Scottish name, just like mine."

Albert regarded him dully. "Aren't you a little young to be putting on airs?" he asked.

Harry felt as if he'd been punched in the stomach. "What?" he asked, bewildered.

Albert continued, "You're only—what?—a year older than me, at most, and you're starting at this crappy place, and you're acting like you've just joined the board of some big corporation. A little pretentious, don't you think?"

It's all true, thought Harry, ready as always to believe bad things about himself. A portion of life left his body, seemingly never to return.

"Albert, stop it!" Bernice ordered. "He was just being polite. You're going to get fired if you don't shape up."

"I was just stating a fact," said Albert officiously.

Suddenly, a voice came from the hall—not a voice, really, but a howl of ultimate pain and rage. "Goddamnit, where is he?" it cried. "I'll kill him!"

"Uh-oh," said Albert unconcernedly. "Trouble."

"Where is that white motherfucker?" the voice said. The door burst open and the voice's owner, a bald young black man with the compact frame of a middleweight boxer, came charging in, eyes aflame. "It was you, wasn't it?" he said, pointing to Albert. "You put condoms on my hot dogs! I'm going to kill your white ass!"

At the words, "You put condoms on my hot dogs," all of the spectators burst into varying degrees of laughter. Harry laughed the loudest of all; something broke within him, and the laughter flowed loudly and deeply.

"Stop laughing!" the angry young man cried. "You did it, didn't you?"

Albert replied languidly, "I didn't want you to go eating strange food without protection, Frank. You could catch a sexually transmitted disease."

"Goddamnit, I'll kill you!" he screamed.

"Oh, stop it, both of you!" Bernice said through her laughter.

"What are all of you niggers up to?" someone asked.

Everyone fell silent. Harry, startled at being called a nigger—or that anyone else would use that word in a work environment—turned and saw a young black woman's face looking through the open door. Her large dark brown eyes might have been cannonballs flying at all of them; her dark skin, a strong leather armor; her short straight hair, a helmet.

"Oh, shit," Bernice muttered.

CHAPTER THREE

"What's going on?" the young woman demanded.

"Uh—just a little dispute, Sally," Bernice said. "Nothing major."

"Yeah, well, it's too major for me," Sally replied. She withdrew her head behind the door, and the door closed. Bernice sighed with relief. "Thank God," she said.

"Who was she?" Harry asked in a trembling voice.

"Sally Mayhew, the manager," Bernice replied.

"The biggest bitch who ever drew breath," Richard added, "or hasn't been laid in ten years."

"Oh, she gets laid all the time," Denise rejoined. "No one's ever said 'no' to her, is what her problem is."

"She was the *manager*?" Harry asked, astonished.

Bernice nodded. "Yeah. Now do you see why everyone's so miserable around here?"

Harry's unease gave way to a moment of pure terror. That woman had power over him? His nerves sang with fear. Then something occurred to him. "How come she never interviewed me for this job?" he asked Bernice. "Why were you the one who interviewed me?"

"Oh, she said she was 'too busy.' Which is bullshit. She has plenty of time. She's just lazy, is her problem."

The one called Frank, who had been the picture of blind rage a moment before, was now the soul of affability, and he said, "Yeah, she is bad news. But hey, are you the new assistant sales manager?"

"Yes, I am," Harry replied.

He stuck his hand out. "Pleased to meet you! I'm Frank. Frank Wilson."

"Uh—I'm Harry McCreedy," Harry said, and shook Frank's hand.

"Are you freaked out about how I acted just now? Don't be. I just have a bad temper and fly off the handle a lot. It don't mean nothing. This dude here provokes me a lot," he added, pointing to Albert.

"I've got to keep the old man on his toes," Albert said.

"'Old man,' my ass! I'm only twenty-eight. And how old are you, Harry—thirty or something?"

"No, I'm only twenty-two," Harry replied.

"Oh, good! We don't need some old man coming in here and messing things up. Sales is a young person's job, right, Bernice?"

"Right," Bernice replied, her voice heavy with sarcasm.

"This isn't my only job," Frank continued. "I'm also a minister—I used to be, anyway."

Harry wanted to cry, "What!" But he merely said, "You are?"

"Yes. I was a minister with the Free Will Gospel Church. Started when I was fifteen. What church do you go to, Harry?"

"Frank!" Bernice said. "Stop trying to convert people! Leave him alone! He just got here."

"Oh, I don't mind answering," Harry said. "I go to Old St. Mary's Church, in Chinatown."

"Then what are you—Catholic? Episcopalian?"

"Catholic."

"Well, that's okay. We've got time to work on that."

"FRANK!" Bernice cried.

"Okay, okay, Bernice, you know so much about Jesus, you get to run things. You'll see the error of your ways one day. Me, I've got to do inventory. I'm out of here." He turned back to Albert. "But *you* are buying me lunch today."

"Sure thing, Frank," the youth replied.

"Two hot dogs. With mustard and relish. Just like the ones you ruined."

"Sure thing."

"Good," Frank said, and left the room.

An instant later, Sally reappeared. "You're the new assistant, aren't you?" she asked, pointing to Harry.

"Uh—yes, I am," he stammered.

"Well, come to my office," she said. "I need to talk to you."

"Good luck," Bernice muttered under her breath.

Harry followed Sally down one hall and then another to her office. "I'm Sally Mayhew," she said, flashing an excessively friendly smile.

"Harry McCreedy."

"Nice to meet you, Harry. Where are you from—Boston?"

Harry tried to chuckle, but it came out as a nervous titter. "How can you tell?"

"The funny way you talk, that's how. Here we are." They reached her office and walked in.

"Sit down," she said. "I'm glad you're here. We've been needing a new assistant sales manager. We're always understaffed. Assistant managers don't seem to last long around here."

I wonder why, Harry thought.

"Except for Bernice," Sally continued, "but she only stayed on because she's got no ambition. But you seem like you've got ambition."

"Why—thank you," said Harry, flattered.

"And you've got a degree from a good college, so you're a lot smarter than any of the idiots around here, except maybe for Richard."

"Well, I don't know about that."

Sally gave him a puzzled look. "What do you mean?"

"Well, I've probably got more schooling than most of them, but education has nothing to do with intelligence. Intelligence is knowing how to deal with people."

"Don't make excuses for them," she said. "They're stupid, that's what they are."

"Well, I don't know—"

Sally's eyes bulged from her head; a hard look came into their dark depths. "Are you contradicting me?" she asked in a low, threatening voice.

"Why—no," Harry stammered. "I just..."

"Then maybe you ain't so smart, are you?" she said. "Maybe you're just as dumb as the rest of these dumb niggers."

"I—"

"Don't interrupt!" she demanded, pounding her desk. "I'm the manager here, and you'll do what I say! Is that clear?"

"Yes!" Harry blurted out. Sweat had broken out on his forehead, his cheeks, and the back of his neck. "Yes. Of course you're in charge."

"Good," she said, and her anger subsided. "I know you're new here, and this first week or so you'll only be learning the ropes, but I want you to remember some things."

"Certainly," Harry replied. With trembling hands he took out his handkerchief and wiped his face and neck, then took out his fountain pen and small notebook.

"What are you doing?" Sally asked.

"Uh—writing down what you say," he replied.

"No, you're not. You're going to look at me when I talk to you."

"Uh—what?" Harry, thoroughly bewildered, could not help asking.

"I said look at me when I'm talking to you. Don't you understand English?"

"Uh—yes," Harry said, and rapidly put away his pen and notebook.

"Then why didn't you do what I said right away?"

"I…" Harry could not speak.

"Are you defying me your first morning on the job?" she asked.

"Oh, no, no," Harry stammered. "I just…" Again he fell silent.

"I'm sick and tired of all you uppity niggers," she said. "Get out."

Harry found his voice. "What?" he asked.

"I said, get out! Jesus, you are stupid, even if you do got a degree from a good school."

Can she do this? Harry wondered.

Sally rose from her chair. "I said get out! Now! Or do I have to throw you out?"

Harry got to his feet. "No, no! I'll leave. I just…I don't know." He hung his head.

Sally pointed to the door. "Get…the fuck…out!"

Harry crept out sideways, like a crab, and closed the door.

As soon as he reached the safety of the hallway, he again broke out in a sweat, this time all over his body. His body felt hollow, and the song of fear that his nerves sang echoed throughout its dark chasm. He leaned against the wall for support and mopped his forehead with his handkerchief.

Bernice, who had been waiting in the hall, came up. "She gave you the works, huh?" she asked.

"She's...what's *wrong* with her?" Harry asked.

"She's just mean all the way through," Bernice said. "Don't let her bother you. You'll get used to it—trust me."

St. Michael, Harry prayed, *were you listening to what I said a little while ago?*

CHAPTER FOUR

Harry's first week on the job passed quickly. He found that he could pick up on the way things were done at Port Arthur easily; perhaps he would not fail at this job after all. And he loved the relative freedom that it provided. One was always in motion, moving from one part of the vast showroom to another, or from the showroom all the way back to the even more cavernous warehouse. Port Arthur Shoes was indeed a wide-open space, and its workers could range about almost at will.

For the remainder of that first week, Harry had little contact with Sally, for which he was grateful. He needed time to think up a way of dealing with her. But he was with Bernice and the rest of his coworkers every moment, and they proved an equal source of anxiety. It wasn't that they were poor workers; all of them handled customers skillfully, and some—particularly Denise and Frank—were outstanding. But as soon as the customers left, the bandage of normalcy was ripped off and the enmity beneath oozed, like a suppurating wound, to the surface.

Harry realized that, in order to deal with the situation (if that was possible), he would have to understand its exact nature; and so he set about observing these strange people closely, to learn why they felt the way they did, and who hated whom.

Denise was not, contrary to what Albert always said, crazy; she simply could not stop talking, and sex was her favorite topic. She was always asking Harry how many women he had slept with, what his favorite sexual positions were, and so forth. Harry said that he didn't like to discuss such topics, and anyway, he didn't know her well enough to feel comfortable discussing them with her. Still, Denise pressed on, giving Harry no quarter. She was obsessed with other bodily functions as well—she cut short one inquisition by pulling a sanitary napkin from her pocket and saying, "Excuse me. I've got to go change my filter."

Richard presented a more difficult puzzle. A superficial analyst could point out the obvious causes of his depression— the failure of his marriage, his abandonment of his profession, his fear of aging. But Harry sensed a deeper reason for this man's despair, one concealed in his soul like a forgotten memento in an attic trunk. Richard was a brilliant man, and Harry liked to lunch with him and talk about history, books, and art. It seemed a great injustice that he should be mired in apathy and despair, and in this treacherous place, forever.

In many ways, Albert seemed, in Richard's phrase, simply a "snot-nosed kid," but there was a calculation to his snottiness, a gleam in his eyes as he delivered his putdowns that announced, "I didn't have to say this, but I *chose* to." It was no wonder that Frank hated him so; at times Harry could feel stirrings of the same hatred. Albert was always ready to criticize him, to deliver such lines as "So how does it feel to be sixty-five, Harry?" or "I'm glad I dropped out of college; look where your college diploma got you." Harry tried to keep his tongue and his irritation in check, but Albert's remarks hurt and angered him, as Albert could plainly see. Still, there were occasional hints that Albert did not mean everything he said, that his youthful snottiness was a consciously assumed role, not a reflection of his inner soul. "Don't mind me," he said once. "I just say these things because I'm young and think I know everything."

Frank was the greatest enigma of all. When in a good mood, he was pleasant and intensely spiritual; indeed, he was a bit too pleasant. He spoke in a rapid, high-pitched voice to the accompaniment of wildly gesticulating hands, bulging eyes, and ever-nearer lunges toward the person with whom he was speaking. It was almost as if he were in a manic state, although Harry (admittedly no doctor) doubted this was the case. Like Denise, he probably just didn't have much self-control. What bothered Harry the most about Frank was his incessant proselytizing. "You know, Harry, you Catholics aren't in touch with the real spirit of God. You're too hung up on rules and rituals and a lot of shit that isn't in the Bible."

Oh, God, Harry thought. *Another fundamentalist trying to save a Catholic idolater.* He did not like to argue about his Faith or anyone else's, but this particular canard had always irked him. "Everything the Church teaches is in the Bible," he said in what he hoped was not a defensive tone of voice. "Our interpretation of the Bible is just different from yours, that's all."

"Interpretation," Frank said, leaner closer and poking Harry's knee with his finger. "That's the point. The revelation of the Word of God is right there in the Bible. It doesn't need interpretation."

"Well, Frank, aren't you interpreting the Bible?"

"Of course not! I'm just accepting its self-evident truths. It doesn't need no fancy theology. It's just *there*."

Harry sighed. "Frank, we're both Christians. We're both trying to live our Faith. Isn't that enough? There shouldn't be any quarrel between us."

"No, it's not enough," Frank replied, then smiled brightly and continued, in a voice so rapid that Harry could barely make out the words, "But the Lord is with you, Harry. I can feel that. And He won't take you until He's given you every opportunity to save your soul."

"I know He won't," Harry said quietly. "I just hope I don't blow it."

"Oh, you won't. Not if you turn from your idolatrous ways and listen to what He's really saying."

Irritating as it was, Frank's proselytizing paled in significance to another and more disturbing trait, his violent, unpredictable temper. It was bad enough in itself, with its sudden onrushes and equally sudden retreats, but coming from one who professed to be a devout Christian, it was even more troubling. Harry once nervously asked Frank how he could reconcile his violent temper with his faith.

"Sometimes you got to take up a sword and fight if you're saved," Frank replied. "Anger and love are both part of God, and you got to know when to deploy one and when to deploy the other. My mama—she was the most devout and the truest Christian I've ever known in my life. But one day, when she was working at the post office, she overheard one of her coworkers, a black woman, saying, 'Some of us black people really are niggers.' And she went up to her and asked, '*What did you say?*' And the woman said, 'I said some of us black people really are niggers.' And she had a box cutter, my mama did, and she just took it and sliced that woman's neck with it. She stood up for her people, just like God wanted her to."

Harry's face was pale with terror, his eyes wide with astonishment. "What happened to the woman?" he managed to ask.

"Oh, she didn't die, but she didn't tell on my mama. She was too scared of her. And everyone else hated what the woman said, so they didn't tell on mama either. She showed her. I've always carried a boxcutter around with me since I was a kid, in imitation of my mama. You never know when you might need it."

Harry made an excuse and hurried away. For the next few days, the sight of Frank made him feel vulnerable and afraid.

Bernice was the easiest person at Port Arthur to get along with, the most secure and even-tempered. But her soul was not completely tranquil, either. "I don't know how much longer I can take this shit," she told Harry. "I'm losing my mind. I can't sleep at night. I've got indigestion. It's driving me crazy."

Harry remembered what he had been taught in Church: trials are brought upon us so that we can surmount them, with God's grace, and thereby show to our persecutors what they long to see—God's Spirit working through us. That was a wonderful goal, and if everyone followed that commandment, then the world would seem like Heaven. Harry believed this teaching, but doubted that he could follow it. He was too weak, too erring, to help bring about anything wonderful like that. But he could try to endure until his strength gave out. He tried to pray for strength, but his mind could not form the words. All he could think of was an old, facetious prayer that he had once heard an unbeliever utter, one that seemed so fitting to his present situation: *Jesus, save me from Your followers.*

CHAPTER FIVE

That Friday evening, Harry went to the hospital to see his mother. She was tiny and frail at five feet and ninety pounds, and her skin, once flushed with life, now had a dried, malnourished look. Her long, finely chiseled face looked haggard and tired, her pale brown eyes seemed always on the verge of closing in exhaustion, her long and beautiful dark brown hair was scraggly and unkempt. Still, when she raised an arthritic claw that had once been a hand and brushed it against Harry's face, he felt as warm and loved as if she had taken him onto her lap and covered him with hugs and kisses.

"How's the job going, darling?" she asked in her tired, dull voice. The corners of her mouth were raised feebly in a smile.

He sighed. "I've never lied to you, mother," he said, and proceeded to tell her about the bizarre, stressful situation at Port Arthur Shoes.

She frowned, an expression that, in her present state, she could manage better. "I'm so sorry," she said. "But Harry, I know this just sounds like something a mother would say to encourage her son, but I know that you can handle it. Not only that, but I know that you can come out on top. You're a very strong person, much stronger than you give yourself credit for."

"You really think so, mother?" he asked with a child's eagerness.

"Oh, yes. Only a very strong person would try to get me out of this place, and take me in and care for me when I'm such a mess and only have a little while left to live. You're my hero, Harry. I'm so proud of you, and I know that your dad is proud of you, too."

Harry's ducts squeezed out a stream of tears, and he held his mother close for a long time, sobbed, and sniffed her hair. It did not have the old familiar clean smell, but the feel of it tickling his nostrils made up for that.

The next morning, Saturday the eighteenth, Harry sat in a pew at Old St. Mary's during morning Mass and thought of how long he had been kept from his mother, and of how short a time it would be before she was taken away from him again. He did not rebel against this; any amount of time that he could spend with her, no matter how brief, was a blessing. To complain was a luxury for those who had never been kept from a loved one, and who expected the blessings of life to last forever.

You're my hero. His mother had meant those words from the bottom of her heart. He was only a weak and paltry hero, of course, come to save a weak and paltry heroine, but it must mean something to God, and to the history of the world as a whole. She was his mother, and had taught him to love, and to recognize and catch life's quicksilver joys. What else could he do but try to save her?

As Harry brooded, the priest went on with the Mass. This church offered the old Latin Mass, thank God, not that modern whitewashed vernacular travesty that passed for a Mass. Usually, Harry followed the Mass very closely, and took time to reflect upon the meaning of each phrase and action, but this morning his thoughts were elsewhere. He barely noticed even when the priest placed the Host upon his tongue. His thoughts followed but one familiar track: *Please help mother and me. Please help us.*

CHAPTER SIX

As he often did on weekends, Harry went from church to the downtown Barnes and Noble bookstore. Since it was a beautiful fall day, he walked instead of taking the subway there. Once inside, he looked through his favorite sections—literature, drama, and history—while keeping an eye out for attractive women. He loved to observe women, but that was usually as far as he got with them. But this morning there were no interesting-looking women in the store, so Harry concentrated his full attention on book finding. A short while later, however, as he was browsing through the history section, he suddenly became aware of a tall woman walking down the aisle toward him. He turned and looked at her.

The woman was slender and, upon closer inspection, above average in height rather than tall. Her skin had a dark, olive complexion: a full-blooded Italian, no doubt. Her dark brown hair was thick and straight, and extended down her back almost to the level of her full, rounded breasts. Her face was long and rectangular, with a high forehead overhanging a flat nose and prominent cheeks, which in turn overhung a strong chin. Her pale green eyes were deep-set and ethereal. Her face was unwrinkled, but Harry could tell that she was much older than he was; in her thirties, perhaps even forty. Still, she forced herself upon his consciousness with singular violence.

Suddenly their eyes met, and Harry forced himself to give her a confident smile. In return, she gave him a wide, toothy smile that exposed two rows of large, straight, shiny white teeth. Harry was smitten.

The woman—who was wearing, he now noted, an old-fashioned, ladylike white dress with a plaid skirt—walked past him, then stopped a few paces away and began to peruse the shelves. He had to talk to her—but how to begin?

Harry noted with gratitude that the book she had taken from the shelf—a dual biography of kings Richard III and Henry VII of England—was one that he had read. Seizing his opportunity, he remarked, "That's a good book."

The woman looked at him and smiled the same toothy smile as before. "Is it?" she asked. Her voice was high and cheerful, and while it had no traceable accent, Harry guessed that she came from somewhere in the Northeast, New York probably.

"Yes, it's an excellent book," Harry went on, his shyness overmastered by his determination to speak.

The woman lowered her head. "Thanks for the advice," she said, her voice sinking to a whisper.

With a start Harry realized that the woman was as shy as he was! It didn't seem possible; this woman was too pretty, too mature, and carried about her too much of a vague air of accomplishment, to be shy. Yet she was. She belonged to the same benighted fraternity as he. Now he simply *had* to speak with her. "You know, there's that big controversy about whether or not Richard III was a great villain or a good king, and whether Henry VII was a savior or a tyrant who usurped Richard's crown and murdered the princes in the Tower," Harry said, lapsing into a professorial mode. "And most of the books on both men spend most of their time trying to argue one side or the other. That book stuck with the facts, and tried to consider both sides of the argument."

"Are you a history teacher?" the woman asked. "You sound like one."

Harry chuckled. "Well, I once wanted to be. But I changed my mind and changed my major to business."

"Oh, really? What do you do?"

"I'm one of the assistant sales managers at the Port Arthur Shoe Store on Pennsylvania Avenue."

"Oh, yes, I pass by that place a lot, but I'm afraid I've never been in there."

Harry could not feign confidence for long, and he frowned and lowered his head. "Well, I'm afraid I haven't been there very long. In fact, I just started there at the beginning of this week. I'm lucky I found it—it took me a few months to find a job here in D.C., and it's been a few months since I got out of college."

Her eyes widened. "You just got out of college? My goodness, I thought that you were older."

Harry looked up and began to relax. "Well, thank you. Everyone thinks that, but no, I'm only twenty-two."

She leaned forward into his space and squinted her eyes as she examined him closely. "Yes, now that I look at you closely, I guess you do look that young. Yet you carry yourself like you were so much older."

"People tell me that," Harry said. "I'm glad of that. I wouldn't want people to think of me as…frivolous, or something."

"You don't at all," the woman said quietly—could she be speaking in admiration? Then she blushed and looked away. "You're really going to be embarrassed when you find out what an old lady you're talking with."

She was actually embarrassed! It didn't seem possible in today's world for people to have such delicate feelings anymore. People who truly felt things deeply didn't seem to stand a chance. People like himself and this woman.

"Nonsense!" Harry said, trying to sound gallant, and succeeding. "It's a pleasure to speak with you."

She looked into his eyes and smiled from her heart. "Well, thank you," she replied, her voice deeper now, almost husky, with choked emotion.

Harry extended his hand. "I'm Harry. Harry McCreedy."

She took his hand by the fingers and raised it to the level of her breasts. "It's so nice to meet you, Harry. I'm Sandra Trefontana."

"Trefontana," Harry mused. "That means 'three fountains.' You know, there's a legend about—"

"—the place in Rome where St. Paul was supposed to have been beheaded," Sandra picked up the thread of conversation, "and his head supposedly bounced three times on the ground, and fountains sprang up at those places. Yes, I know the story. It's very charming, isn't it?"

"Very. And what do you do, Sandra?"

This time her smile was wry. "I'm an executive secretary with the Department of Justice. Can you believe it? I'm a Republican and here I am working for bloated big government."

"Gosh, that's a wonderful job! You shouldn't be embarrassed. I'm a Republican, too, and I don't think that's bad. Someone has to run things, I guess."

"I suppose. But I suppose I should tell you—getting back to the age thing—that not only am I thirty-nine years old, I've never been married. So you're talking to an aging spinster!" She laughed a jagged, nervous laugh. "Are you sure talking to me won't make you lose status in your friends' eyes?"

"I don't have any status," Harry replied with a sad smile.

Sandra gave him a sympathetic look. "You're pretty shy, huh? Join the club." She laid a hand on his arm, and the sensation, coupled with the look of that hand—a little veined with age but still long, thin, strong looking, and covered with smooth olive skin—made Harry instantly, tautly erect. To this lust was coupled another sensation, that of a bond between them based on sympathy and understanding. How long, he wondered, had it been since another person, except for his mother, had treated him with such sympathy and understanding: ten years? A dozen years? Ever?

"What church do you belong to, Harry?" she asked.

"Old St. Mary's in Chinatown."

"That place where they do the old Latin Mass? Cool! So you're a Catholic?"

"Yes."

"This is scary. We've got *too much* in common. My mother and I go to the Basilica."

"Isn't that one of the most beautiful places you've ever seen?"

"Yes, it is." She paused, then giggled as if she were planning something naughty and said, "I was going to get some coffee at the coffee bar. Would you like to join me, Harry?"

Harry's chest swelled with joy. "I'd love to."

They went to the coffee bar and ordered their drinks—a French vanilla cappuccino for Harry, an espresso for Sandra—then sat down at a table by the window. "So how did you get such a neat job, Sandra?" Harry asked.

She frowned. "It's a long story. When I went away to college way back in the dark days of—my goodness, 1977—the year that you were born, isn't that right, Harry?"

"Yes, I was born on April the twentieth of that year." He smiled. "Just before the summer when *Star Wars* was released."

Sandra smiled in turn. "Yes, I remember it well. I've always been a big *Star Wars* fan. What about you, Harry?"

"Oh, yes, but—well, I certainly didn't stand in line for three days to get tickets when the new *Star Wars* film came out this summer."

"Me neither. Did you like the new film?"

"It was all right."

"Yeah, my opinion exactly. Anyway, to get back to my story, when I went away to college—I went a year early, I was a very smart kid—I really didn't know what I wanted to do. I thought for a while about becoming a lawyer—my dad, who's now deceased, was a really big antitrust lawyer. He loved me very much, but he and my mom were always disappointed that I wasn't all filled with get-up-and-go like they were, and I knew that becoming a lawyer would be a way of showing them that I was like them, after all. But then I thought, nah, that's not for me, I'll go into business—just like you did, Harry. But then, one day during the summer of 1979, in between my sophomore and junior years, I went to see *Moonraker*, the James Bond film. Do you know it?"

"Oh, yes, I've seen all the James Bond films."

"It figures. He's every man's secret role model, isn't he?"

"I suppose so."

"Well, anyway, I don't know if you remember the title song to that film—Shirley Bassey sang it, she also sang—"

"—the theme song to *Goldfinger*."

"Right. And anyway, the theme song to *Moonraker* was all about yearning for someone to love you, to really love you and sanctify your life. And as I sat there listening to it, it occurred to me how lonely I really was, how I'd never had any close friends or a real boyfriend or anything like that. And I also thought about how I just couldn't make up my mind about what I wanted to do in life, and about how my parents had always told me,

'Sandra, if you don't get hold of yourself and stop being afraid of life, you're going to be crushed underfoot like a bug. You can't be as weak as you are and survive in this world.' That was fine, but they never told me how *not* to be afraid! And as I was walking home after the movie, I kept thinking over and over, 'It's true. I am going to be crushed. I'm lost, and even God doesn't care about me anymore.' And then, the world...sort of receded. I had this horrendous breakdown. I really don't remember much of what happened between then and the next summer. I was able to get up and do a few things by myself, they told me, but I really don't remember any of it. I came out of it a little the next summer, and you know, it's funny, but that next summer, 1980, the second *Star Wars* film was released, *The Empire Strikes Back*. And one day my mom and I were sitting in the garden of the hospital where I was staying, and for some reason I was fairly lucid that day, and my mom said to me, 'Sandra, I was reading in the paper the other day about the new *Star Wars* movie, and did you know that Darth Vader turns out to be Luke Skywalker's father?' And I actually felt coherent enough to say, 'Mom, you're not supposed to tell me things like that! Now you've ruined the whole movie for me.' That was the start of my recovery. Later on, my parents and I went to see *The Empire Strikes Back* together. That was the first movie I'd seen in a year. And by spring of the next year—1981—I was able to return to college. I finished up in the fall of '82, just a year and a half late, with a degree in Business Administration. And then I went to work as a secretary for bloated big government, and I couldn't believe it! I actually did well, people liked me, and I was earning good money. That went on for six years, and I was just as happy as could be. I also managed to lose my virginity, if that matters. Then one day— I'll never forget it, it was two days before Valentine's Day, 1989— my dad took me to lunch and said, 'Sandra, honey, you're going to be thirty in a year. Don't you think that you should think about doing something more with your life?' Well, with that remark, all of my fears about not being able to cope came back to me in an instant, *whump!* And I passed out. I was out of commission for nine months that time. I remember the first time I was really lucid after that breakdown was on November the ninth, when the news came about the Berlin Wall coming down. That was such good news that I knew it must be a sign from God that He had a future for me. And then, over Christmas, when all of those Communist regimes were collapsing all over the place, I knew for certain that everything was going to be all right. I'd never abandoned my Faith, but for a long time I'd wondered, 'Why did God put me on the earth if I'm so ill-equipped to handle it?' But I've never thought that since then. And I've done pretty well since then, too. It did take me a while to get over my dad's death—he died of a stroke seven years ago—but I didn't have a breakdown. The only other time I've really felt depressed was three years ago, when I developed cancer and had to have a hysterectomy. I took a month off from work to recuperate, so I guess that was a mini-breakdown, of sorts. I wasn't that depressed about not being able to have children any longer—I was a little happy, if you want to know the truth. I know that sounds terrible, but I've never really felt comfortable around children—I guess I'm so shy and have lived within myself for so long that I never really had time to be a kid and get to understand other children."

"I feel the exact same way," Harry said.

"Somehow I knew that. Anyway, I was scared about being so horribly sick and then dying before I was ever really happy in this life. But you know what really terrified me? That I'd have to undergo chemotherapy and lose my hair. This sounds incredibly vain, but my hair is my one great external accomplishment, the one thing about me, externally, that I'm really proud of! And I didn't want to lose that." She picked up a clump of her beautiful dark brown hair, then let its strands slip through her fingers and fall back into place.

"That would have been terrible," Harry said with deep feeling. "You have the most beautiful hair."

She placed her hands on top of his. "Thank you," she said. Something began to work between them, a strange and delightful chemistry that flowed like electricity from the one to the other. "So I prayed to God to let me live and keep my hair—if

He wanted me to, of course—and to be happy in this world and do something good for someone else before I died. Anyway, the hysterectomy took care of my problems—I've had a clean bill of health since then, and the doctor says there's a good chance that the cancer will never return. And I'm an executive secretary now, so I'm making really good money, and my mom and I are really close—she'll never learn to treat me like an adult, but at least she treats me like a teenager now instead of an infant! I'm very fortunate. The only bad thing is—I'm still as shy as I always was, and I still haven't found someone to really love me!" Tears streamed down her face, distorting it; she wiped them away. "Well, that's my whole life story. And I can't believe it. I've never told the whole story before to anyone like that. And here I am telling it to you, a stranger I've just met! And one so much younger than me, too. Why am I doing this? I don't get it."

"I don't know," Harry replied.

Her eyes grew wide with a dawning sense of wonder. "Do you think that maybe we were meant to meet each other? That this is our destiny, somehow?"

"I don't know, but I'm glad we met."

She squeezed his hands. "So am I. Now, tell me your life story."

"Well, it's a very long story," Harry remarked, and did so. He spoke for twenty minutes, first in the coffee bar, then on the bench outside to which they moved in order to enjoy the sunny day. He told her everything, including how, in his adolescence, he had sometimes had to sleep outside because one of his relatives had thrown him out in disgust and another relative-boarder could not be contacted on such short notice. One snowy winter's night he had even had to sleep in his Aunt Susan's car. When he awoke shivering the next morning, the car was completely enveloped in snow, and the look of the snow pressing against the car windows terrified him; it was dirty and gray, the color of ashes, of death and decay. Consequently, the sight of snow had always terrified him. And he told her about his current situation, his plans to rescue his mother, and his plans for the future. And as he related all this, Sandra held him, and occasionally stroked his face, and looked at him with one of the most desolate expressions that Harry had ever beheld.

"Oh, you poor thing," she said when he had finished. "Oh, you poor, poor thing."

This sympathy was so rare in Harry's experience that for an instant he did not know what to do. Then he realized how warm and secure a place was the bosom of one who shows sympathy, and so he laid his head upon Sandra's bosom, and she folded him in her arms, and covered his face with kisses, and wept silently, anointing him with her tears.

Something changed in Harry—an internal gear shifted, his chemistry altered, or his genes mutated into a different pattern, perhaps. At any rate, when he finally left Sandra's embrace, his mind and body could do new things. He kissed her, and she closed her eyes, gave a little shudder, and slid her tongue into his mouth. They held each other tightly, with a desperation and hunger that would have been frightening had it not been so beautiful.

Afterward they had lunch, and went to the National Gallery of Art (Sandra had two free passes), then went back to Harry's apartment and tried to watch a video. But they could not stop kissing and fondling each other, so they stripped off their clothes and explored each other's naked bodies, at first like children examining something strange and new, then like worshippers adoring something holy. Finally they came together, which was easily accomplished—"I love you so much a river's flowing out of me!" Sandra cried—and it took Harry a long time to reach his culmination, which allowed Sandra to reach hers again and again. When it happened for him at last, he felt purged in some savage, hurtful way; the violence of satiation was at least as great as the violence of desire.

Soon they were at it again, and Sandra used her mouth and fingers to pleasure Harry in a way that reduced him to an animalistic state: he screamed and kicked and thrashed like a wild beast consumed with bloodlust. Then he used the tip of his tongue to pleasure her, faithfully following her instructions: circle it slowly, then mash your tongue across it. After a brief nap to recover their strength, they were at it again vigorously; the whole world seemed a place for nothing but thrusting, it was the only effort that could accomplish anything. They did it one more time before their energies were spent, and that final coupling was slow and gentle, and seemed to last for ages. Then they slept some more, with their arms and legs wrapped around each other, and when they awoke, Sandra propped herself up on Harry's chest and let her beautiful hair spill down upon it, and smiled an otherworldly smile.

"I'm a great cook," she said dreamily, "so would you like to come over to my apartment and let me cook you dinner? I live just about ten blocks from here."

"That would be wonderful," he said.

"Will you spend the night with me?"

"Yes."

"The weekend?"

"Yes."

"My mother is out of town this weekend, so can I go to Mass with you tomorrow at your church?"

"I'd love to share that with you."

"And then we can go to lunch...and go for a walk...and rent some videos...and make love some more...and just spend time together."

"I want to do that."

"You'll really hold me close all night? You won't let me go?"

"Not for a minute. Will you hold me?"

"Oh, so close...so close. And then on Monday morning, before we have to get up and go to work, will you make love to me one last time?"

"I sure will."

She touched his face and kissed his mouth. "Please be real," she said.

"I am," he assured her.

CHAPTER SEVEN

The following Monday at work, Denise asked Harry, "Did you get laid last weekend?"

Harry blinked and started. "Uh…why do you ask that?"

"'Cause you act all loose and relaxed, not uptight like you usually do."

"Oh," he stammered. "Well…there could be lots of reasons for that."

"You did get laid, didn't you? And now all that stuff ain't clogging you up, and you're all relaxed, and that steel rod that was rammed up your ass has fallen out! Ain't that what happened?"

The truth was obvious, so he admitted it. "Yes."

"Well, ain't that special! So who is she?"

He smiled. "Someone very special."

"I'm sure she is." Then she called out to the other coworkers in the break room, "Hey, everybody, Harry got laid last weekend!"

"Denise," Harry hissed through clenched teeth.

"What's the big deal?" she asked. "It ain't nothing to be ashamed of."

"Do you have to broadcast it like that?"

"Sure I do! We know everything about everyone's sex life around here."

Richard spoke up from across the room. "Good for you, Harry. It's nice to know that someone's getting some around here."

Frank remarked, "I'm surprised at you, Harry. Not because you're a good Catholic and gave in to lusts of the flesh—all you Catholics do that. It's just that I thought you were queer."

A sudden wave of anger surged through Harry, but was quickly overpowered by one of bewilderment. "Why did you think that?" he asked.

"Because you were so quiet and scholarly and liked artistic things. I always thought that meant a person was queer."

"Well, no, I'm as straight as an arrow."

"Good! Then I don't have to worry about turning you away from that perverted way of life."

"Frank, shut up!" Richard cried, his face and voice dark with rage. "Leave him alone! Why don't you try and take care of your own soul before worrying about everybody else's? Jesus, you're the worst Christian I've ever met."

"All right, be that way," Frank said, and lapsed into a sulky silence.

"Thank you, Richard," Harry said.

"My pleasure."

Albert spoke up. "Well, nice to see you're getting some action, Harry," he said languidly. "And don't worry. *I* never thought that you were gay."

"Well, that's nice," Harry muttered.

Albert smiled wickedly. "Yeah, your ass is too tight to stick anything up it."

A fresh wave of murderous anger came over Harry, and he glared at Albert, who merely shrugged and rolled his eyes innocently. At that moment, Bernice hurried into the break room.

"Bad news," she announced. "Sally is on the warpath. Our sales figures for last week were all screwed up, and there's no way of figuring them out properly."

"I'm not surprised," Harry said, "what with the way they record sales figures around here. It's so inefficient."

"Yeah, that form we have to fill out is a real bitch," Denise said.

"And that computer program we have—it drives me nuts," Bernice added. "It's impossible."

"Those things should be changed," Harry remarked.

"I agree," Bernice said. "But how?"

"Well...if Sally would let me, I could redesign them."

A light of hope dawned in Bernice's eyes. "Harry, could you go and tell Sally that right now, and see if you can talk her into letting you do that before she dumps on all of us?"

Surprised that his chance remark should be taken so seriously, Harry said, "Well, yes. I'll go talk to her." He left the break room and walked to Sally's office, his anxiety growing with each step. *What if this doesn't work?* he thought. *What if it does?*

He knocked on the door of Sally's office, and she yelled "Come in!" with such violence that Harry recoiled and paused before entering. She was seated at her computer and pounding at the keyboard with such violence that Harry was certain the keys would break. "What do you want?" she demanded.

Harry's facial muscles twitched, and he swallowed. "I…understand that last week's sales figures are all screwed up," he said quietly.

"Yes, they are! Thanks to these fucking idiots. What's it got to do with you?"

"Uh…well, I think I know how we can make sure that doesn't happen again."

"How? By getting a gun and shooting the fools?"

"No, by redesigning the computer program we use to—uh—input the data, and by rewriting the form that we use to record it. It can be made much simpler, and shorter. It's two pages long and has way too many questions. You could make it much shorter."

"And who's going to do that?"

His facial muscles twitched again. "Well…I could give it a try."

Her sarcastic rage softened a little. "You? You mean you actually want to try to make things better around here?"

"Why—yes!" said a bewildered Harry.

She regarded him suspiciously for a moment, then said, "Okay, college boy, you want the job, you got it. You got two days to rewrite the form and redesign the program." She pointed a finger at him. "But you got *only* two days. And don't go implementing nothing until I approve it."

"Two days is more than enough time," Harry said.

"Great."

"I'll get right to work."

"Just one thing," Sally said. "Did those damned fools send you here to talk to me?"

"Uh…yes," Harry admitted.

"You made these suggestions and they sent you over here to try them out on me, didn't they?"

"Well, yes, they did," Harry admitted, his stomach knotting up, his burgeoning sense of triumph seemingly in danger of being slain in the cradle.

"It figures. Well, I like your ideas, so I'll give them a chance. But I'm doing it for the sake of the company, not to let those fucking idiots off the hook."

Harry shuddered. She doesn't even want them to do better, he thought. She enjoys it when they screw up, because then she can feel superior to them. She enjoys being angry. She enjoys chaos. What kind of a human being is she?

"Well, get to work," Sally ordered.

"I will," Harry promised, and left her office.

Outside in the hallway, Harry took in a deep breath and let it out. He felt lighter all of a sudden, giddy not with triumph, but with the possibility of triumph. He had taken hold of this terrible situation and would try to change it. He was attempting an incredibly aggressive and daring thing. It didn't seem possible.

I don't know why You're still looking after me, he told God, *but thank You anyway.*

CHAPTER EIGHT

Harry redesigned the program and rewrote the form in just over a day, and Sally was, albeit reluctantly, impressed. His changes were adopted, and by the beginning of the following week, they began to show results: not only were the sales figures wholly accurate and in impeccable order for the first time in living memory, but the process of recording and tabulating them had been accomplished in record time. "Thanks for the good work," Sally said, and gave him a little smile.

Harry's coworkers were more fulsome in their praise. "You saved us," Bernice said. "That was one of the things that bitch always got onto us about. I don't know what she'll do now that she doesn't have that to complain about." Richard's remarks meant even more to Harry. "This is the first time that someone's actually *done* something around here that I can remember!"

So the world, while always ready with another hammer-blow, was not completely invincible. He had made his first mark upon the world; for the first time he had forced it, albeit in a small way, to bend to his will. Perhaps he would not be crushed underfoot like a bug, after all. He sent up a little prayer of thanks-giving.

His personal life was even more glorious. At last he could express his damned-up feelings of love and desire and affection, and to someone worthy; he loved and was loved. Sandra and he spent every night and all of their spare time together. Their new union seemed the natural order of things; even their bodies knew this, for they could not sleep until they had wrapped their arms and legs around each other. Love was something you deserved, it was the way things should be! It didn't seem possible.

Physical love liberated them in a different way. All that was aggressive and daring in their natures was cut loose; every thrust and kiss and touch and yearning look seemed to free them a little more from the bonds of fear, hesitancy, and shyness. Denise was right—it did loosen him up, and Sandra too. Having sex outside of marriage made them feel somewhat guilty—or, more precisely, it made them feel that they *should* feel guilty—but their lust was too great, and had been too long deferred, for them to do anything now but surrender to it.

Harry had already made up his mind that at Christmas, if some horrible catastrophe had not taken Sandra away from him, then he would ask her to marry him. Then they would reach that later, deeper stage of love, the sacrament blessed by God. But for now they were in the first giddy stage of love, beside themselves with joy, and in no particular hurry to go anywhere.

CHAPTER NINE

The job at Port Arthur Shoes carried a generous life and health insurance policy with it, which was one reason why Harry had been so pleased to get the position. After a couple of weeks on the job, he finally received his insurance and prescription cards, and felt weak in the knees with gratitude. Now he could pay for his mother's medicine and her doctor's visits himself. At last he could get her out of that wretched charity hospital while she still had some life left within her. He thought of how the people there had allowed her heart condition to go undiagnosed until it was too late to do anything about it, and felt a momentary flash of rage. But he realized that such wrath was foolish and self-indulgent; he needed to get his mother out of that hellhole, and that was all that mattered. If there was to be any redemption in this entire heartbreaking affair, then he must enable her to finish her life in freedom, surrounded by love. One had to forgive, and move on. Besides, if love and happiness were the light at the end of this long dark tunnel, then it would be much easier to forgive.

His mother was frightened at the idea of getting out of the hospital. "I've been away so long, baby," she told Harry, "that I'm just not sure I can cope anymore."

"You won't have to cope, mother," he assured her. "I'll take care of you. All you'll have to do is be happy and live...well...live...for as long as you can."

"Harry, I'm sorry," she said quietly. "I always knew that you were a good, loving person, but I never realized how good and loving you were until now. I'm sorry I didn't realize it earlier. Then I could have loved you more."

Harry smiled and kissed his mother, and then told her about Sandra. At this news her eyes showed more happiness and animation than they had for over a decade. "Oh, I'm so glad," she whispered. "Oh, thank You, Jesus, thank you, Blessed Mother."

"I'm glad you're so happy about it," Harry said.

"Oh, that's the best news I've ever heard in my life. I—

well, I suppose I can't know the future, but if this works out like it sounds that it will, then I can die happy. I'll know you'll be safe."

"Because I'll have someone to take care of me?" Harry asked, smiling.

"Well, yes, of course, but more important, you'll have someone to love and to love you back. You're such a loving person—you can't spend your life with no one to share that love with."

"Yes," Harry said. "You're sure you approve? I mean, she is a lot older than me."

"Sweetheart, why would I care about that? You love each other and can give to each other. That's what's important. I know that sounds like a silly idealistic thing to say, but it's true."

"I'm so glad. And...you don't mind that she's suffered from depression?"

She gave a chuckle that actually had enough strength and volume to resemble a genuine laugh. "Harry, I hardly think that I'm entitled to look down on someone because they've had psychological problems."

"Well, yes, but once you told me that you hoped I would find someone who didn't have problems like you did—that you'd let me down and couldn't do anything for me, and that I should find someone healthy who could do things for me, whom I wouldn't have to look after."

"I know, darling, but she can do things for you, and you can do things for her. Maybe God put you in her life so that she won't have to suffer like I did—if she has another breakdown, I mean, which I pray to God she won't. Love isn't about security—love is about helping each other and giving to each other. That's the kind of love your father and I had...and I see that you and I have, too."

Harry hugged his mother so tight that she cried, "Oof! You're crushing me!"

"Oh, my gosh!" he said. "I forgot you're so fragile! Oh, mother, I'm so sorry!"

"Don't be, silly!" she replied, and stroked his cheek.

When Harry got home that evening, Sandra was waiting

for him with dinner. He told her what his mother had said, and she began to sob. Harry tried to comfort her, but it was a long time before his words and ministrations had any effect.

Later that night, as they lay in each other's arms, Sandra suddenly asked, "Harry—I want so much to meet your mother, but could I go and meet her the first time by myself? I want to talk to her about some things, and I'd—rather talk to her alone."

"Why, certainly, honey," he said.

"You're sure it doesn't seem too pushy? I mean, she's your mother. I don't want to just insert myself into her life without your knowing about it."

Harry rubbed up against her and fondled her breasts. "All I care about is inserting myself into *your* life."

She laughed and shoved him. "*Stop* it, you pervert, I'm serious!"

"I know, darling. But no, that's perfectly all right. I know you have a...traumatic experience in common, and that you'd want to talk about that with her yourself."

Sandra laughed again. "You mean we were crazy? Come on, Harry, say it. We were crazy. We went nuts."

"All right, you were crazy. But go ahead and see her. I'm sure she'd love it."

"Good. I just didn't want to seem like a pushy female. I know if there's one thing men hate, it's pushy females."

"I'd never think that of you, Sandra."

"Good." She began to rub up against him and to lick his ears. With one hand she grasped him, effecting an immediate change. "Were you serious about inserting yourself into my life?" she asked.

He moaned in reply.

"Good," she whispered, and guided him in the fulfillment of his desire.

The next day after work, Sandra went to the charity hospital. As she asked for directions to Harry's mother's room, her heart pounded in her chest, and her nerves tingled. While this place was much worse than the hospitals that she had stayed in during her two breakdowns, it still evoked those horrible memories. But she was overwrought for another reason, as well: she was going into this hellhole to do something good for, to make a connection with, a fellow sufferer. She felt almost as if she were on a mission to rescue Harry's mother, one with only a slim chance of success.

She took the elevator up to the fourth floor and walked down the corridor until she found the room. The door was open, and Harry's mother was sitting in a cheap aluminum chair by the window, reading a book. Sandra stood in the doorway for a moment, then swallowed and asked, "Mrs. McCreedy?"

The older woman looked up, perplexed. "Yes?"

"Hello. I'm sorry to barge in on you unannounced, but I'm Sandra Trefontana, Harry's girlfriend. I wanted to drop by and see you, and—here I am!"

The mother's expression changed to one of as much delight as her depleted strength would allow. "Oh, how wonderful. Please come in and have a seat."

Sandra pulled up a chair and sat down beside Harry's mother, and took one of her hands in both of hers. "I'm so glad to meet you," she said.

"I am, too," Mrs. McCreedy replied. "You know, I've only known you for a minute, but I can see why Harry loves you so much. You're very sweet and loving, just like he said."

Sandra blushed. "Thank you."

"And you're even more beautiful than he said you were."

She blushed deeper, lowered her head, and could not speak for a moment. When she had found her voice again, she said, "Mrs. McCreedy—the reason I came to see you by myself is— Harry told you that I've suffered from depression, like you have, didn't he?"

"Yes, he told me about it."

"Well, right now you're in the position that I used to be in—and you're going to get out of it very soon, thank God—but since we both went through the same thing, there's that additional connection between us besides Harry. I wanted to tell you about what I went through because—well, I know you'd understand."

Harry's mother laid a hand on Sandra's arm. "Of course, Sandra. Please tell me about it."

And Sandra did, leaving nothing out. When she had finished, Mrs. McCreedy took Sandra's strong, smooth hands in her enfeebled claws. "I'm sorry about your losing your father and your uterus...and your cancer scare," she said. "But honey, you've been given several wonderful chances in your life. You got over depression twice, you got over cancer, and now you've met a man who really loves you. You should get down on your knees every day and thank God for all of your blessings."

"Oh, I do, Mrs. McCreedy, I thank Him a hundred times *every* day for all of that."

The mother smiled. "Good girl. I wish I'd been as blessed as you. But no, though I've been in the hospital and away from Harry and the world for twelve years, I'm still blessed, because now I'm getting out and I'm going to be able to spend my life— well, what's left of it, I don't have much time left, you know— with you and Harry. If the ending is so wonderful, I don't care about what happened before."

"Oh, Mrs. McCreedy!" Sandra cried, and pulled Harry's mother to her.

Mrs. McCreedy let Sandra cry herself out. Then she said, "Sandra, my name's Elizabeth. You can call me Elizabeth if you like."

Sandra wiped away her tears and looked the older woman in the eyes. "Absolutely not," she declared. "You're Harry's mother, and you deserve to be treated with respect."

"Well, that's sweet, but honey, you're what, thirty-nine? I'm only eleven years older than you."

"I don't care if you're eleven years younger. I'm a proper Catholic girl, and I'm supposed to treat my boyfriend's mother with respect. You've had too little respect in your life, Mrs. McCreedy. And you deserve to be treated with respect. I'm calling you Mrs. McCreedy, and that's *final.*"

Mrs. McCreedy chuckled. "You're spunky on top of everything else. That's delightful. All right, Sandra. But, listen...could you please do me a favor?"

"Anything, darling. What is it?"

"You know that, for a long time, Harry's father's family basically—" she flinched at the memory "—kept him from seeing me very often once I was hospitalized?"

"Yes, and that was an absolute *sin*," Sandra said fiercely.

"Don't let hatred control your life, Sandra. It's—it's the great destroyer. But listen. Harry is so happy now that he can take care of me and do something for me. Before, of course, there was only so much that he could do, but not being able to do *anything* for me at all just tore the poor thing's heart out. Now, I pray that you'll never suffer a breakdown again or even feel depressed for one second more, but…if that ever should happen…do you promise that you'll let Harry take care of you? If another person he loved was in trouble and he couldn't do anything to help, I think it would kill him. Do you promise me that?"

"Oh, yes, Mrs. McCreedy, yes! I don't think I could stop him."

Harry's mother closed her eyes and let out most of the breath in her body. "I'm so glad," she whispered.

Sandra continued, "But listen, honey, as long as I'm healthy, I'm going to help take care of Harry. I'm going to do things for him. I'm not just going to take. You won't have to worry about him when you're…gone…he'll be loved and well taken care of with me."

"Oh, thank You, Jesus," Mrs. McCreedy intoned in a barely audible whisper. "Oh, thank You, thank You, thank You."

Sandra hugged the older woman and felt as if she herself had been liberated from this prison; she felt free, so full of life and rude animal health that it would take several lifetimes to exhaust it all.

"You know, Sandra," Harry's mother said, "I've only known you for half an hour or so, but I feel as if I've known you my whole life. Do you feel that way, too?"

"Yes, Mrs. McCreedy, I do," Sandra replied, and wiped away a tear.

CHAPTER TEN

Sandra's mother Evelyn reacted to the news of her daughter's romance with a great frown. "Sandra," she said after a moment's pause, "I know you're getting older and you're probably depressed about turning forty soon and still being single, and I know that forty is supposed to be the year that women peak sexually, but honestly, this just seems—so foolish."

"Oh, mom, it's not that," Sandra said. "He's a special person."

"How? Because he's young and pays attention to you?"

"No, because he's so sweet and loving. He doesn't seem that young, really—in many ways, he seems a lot older than I am. He's so smart, and he wants to make something of himself, and he's—so different. After a while, people start to seem the same—it's so nice to meet someone who's different, special."

"Sandra, does this have something to do with the fact that you can't have children anymore? Does that make you depressed, and so you're going out with this boy so that you can feel that you really *do* have children, somehow? You loved your father—couldn't you have a father complex instead and go out with some older man?"

"Mom!" Sandra cried, her frustration mounting, tears coming to her eyes.

"I'm sorry, honey. I know I promised your doctors that I'd treat you like an adult. But honestly…people who do these things, it's just a phase with them. You act like it's the romance of the century."

Sandra smiled brightly. "Oh, it is, mom, it is."

"I give up," her mother said.

"Mom, let me tell you about Harry. He comes from a very good old New England family."

"Really?" her mother asked, her interest suddenly piqued.

"Oh, yes. Well, unfortunately, there were some very bad circumstances that happened to him, they weren't his fault, and so…" She sighed, tried to steel herself, and told her the story of

Harry's family.

"Oh, Lord," Mrs. Trefontana said. "The poor fellow. Well, the fact that he wants to establish himself without his family's help, that shows that he has guts."

Sandra felt a sudden wave of joy; was she getting through to her mother? "Yes, it does. And he's a Republican, a very active one—"

Her mother cut in. "Who does he support in the next election?"

"Steve Forbes."

"Well, he's right about that. Is he a Catholic?"

"Oh, yes. He goes to Mass just about every day. He goes to Old St. Mary's, because they do the old Latin Mass there. He's a traditionalist."

Although she tried to stifle her enthusiasm, Mrs. Trefontana was very impressed. "Well, maybe you're right, Sandra. He does seem like a fine young man. Of course, I don't know that what he feels for you isn't just a typical case of a young man letting his hormones get the better of his brain. I'll tell you what. You can bring him over for dinner some evening, and I'll get to know him."

"Mom, you're not going to give him the third degree, are you?" Sandra asked, horrified.

Mrs. Trefontana grinned mischievously. "Of course I am. Don't you know your mother by now?"

So, on the evening of the first Saturday and the second day in October, Sandra and Harry prepared to have dinner at her mother's home. As they were dressing, Sandra went up to Harry and pressed herself against him. "Don't be nervous, darling," she told him. "Mom's really not so bad as she seems—sometimes."

"I'll be okay," said Harry nervously.

"Do you want to make love before we go? Would that make you feel better?"

"No, that's all right, honey."

She frowned. "Well, could we make love anyway? It would make *me* feel better."

So they did, then got dressed and drove to a house in a

quiet, tree-shrouded suburb of Arlington. As they stood at the door, Sandra paused for a moment before ringing the bell. "Are you all right?" she asked Harry.

He smiled nervously. "As all right as I can be under the circumstances."

She smiled in turn. "I can feel your semen inside me. That'll give me courage."

She rang the bell, and within a few seconds Mrs. Trefontana opened the door. Harry looked her over carefully and liked what he saw. Except for her somewhat dry and wrinkled skin and the streaks of gray that had overmastered her brown hair, Mrs. Trefontana was an exact replica of her daughter. He had often heard that a woman's mother was a reliable indicator of how the woman would look in twenty or thirty years. If that was so, then he wouldn't mind growing old with Sandra. Not at all.

"Hello, kids," Mrs. Trefontana said in her thick Brooklyn accent. "Come on in."

"Hello, Mrs. Trefontana," Harry said, extending his hand. "I'm Harry McCreedy."

"Nice to meet you, Harry," she said, and shook his hand. Her skin and handshake felt enough like Sandra's to give Harry a twinge of desire.

After they had stepped into the living room and been seated, Harry remarked, "You have a lovely place here."

"Really?" Mrs. Trefontana asked. "In what way?"

"Well, your taste in furnishing is very Victorian, and I like that, but also, everything seems to be in its proper place. The way you've decorated it doesn't look ostentatious, but then it doesn't look barren either. Everything seems to be in its proper place."

"Well, thank you. That was the effect I was shooting for. I asked you because I wanted to be sure that you really meant what you said. That sounded like a groveling remark, and if there's one thing I can't stand, it's a groveler."

"Oh, Mom," Sandra said.

"So, Harry, Sandra tells me that you're very strong in the Faith."

"Well, I—try, ma'am. People say I'm very devout, but really, I just—keep on trying, no matter how badly I might keep screwing things up."

"Good answer. No one is perfect, you just have to keep on plugging ahead. That's all the Lord expects of us. And she tells me that you're a Steve Forbes supporter."

"Yes, ma'am, I am."

"Good, so am I. And you keep calling me 'ma'am,' so you have good manners."

"Mom, *please* stop making this sound like an inquisition," Sandra begged.

"Sandra, you said that you and Harry had an adult relationship. Your begging me to give him special treatment doesn't sound very much like an adult relationship to me."

Sandra grunted in frustration and turned to Harry. "I'm sorry, Harry," she said. "She just likes to intimidate people. It's a power thing with her. Please don't let her intimidate you."

"You're treating him like a child," Mrs. Trefontana said brightly, as if she had just been proven right.

Harry forced himself to speak, although stress had reduced the volume of his voice. "That's all right, honey. Mrs. Trefontana, I understand this must seem a little strange to you, but rest assured I—Sandra and I really love each other. We really do have an adult relationship—well, goodness knows I don't feel like an adult some of the time, but with Sandra I do. We're partners, equals."

Sandra, delighted with his reply, squeezed his arm and kissed him.

"Well, that's good," Mrs. Trefontana said, conceding defeat. "I hope it's true."

"Oh, it is, Mrs. Trefontana. I'm an honest person."

"Yes, somehow I feel that you are," she said. Harry felt a brief surge of joy: had he won her over? She continued, "So, Harry, Sandra tells me that you come from a fine old family."

"Yes, I do."

"What's your ancestry? Scottish?"

"Well, about fifty percent Scottish, thirty percent English, and twenty percent Irish."

"Well, the Scottish part is great," she said. "The English—well, they're a bunch of effete snobs, but that's all right. The Irish part is bad, very bad, but I guess it's not a big enough part of your heritage to be a real problem."

"Mom!" Sandra cried.

"Sandra, you didn't grow up in the Italian ghetto in Brooklyn, right next to the Irish ghetto. You didn't have to fight your way through the Irish ghetto every time you wanted to go downtown. I swear, I wonder why the Italians and the Irish haven't killed each other off by now."

Harry didn't know what to say. Mrs. Trefontana came to his rescue with another question. "One thing I need to ask you, Harry. You're not slumming, are you?"

"Uh…beg pardon?" he asked.

"You're not slumming, are you? I mean, you have this hoity-toity Boston accent and all, and though I understand you come from a…well…discredited branch of your family, still, in my experience, people from your part of the world tend to look down on most other people. I mean, Sandra's father and I were New York wops who made good, the first generation to do that. You don't see going out with Sandra as just wallowing in the mud for a while with the common folk, do you?"

"Mrs. Trefontana, that never crossed my mind," he replied.

Sandra regarded her mother with open-mouthed astonishment. "Why, mom, you—you mean that, for the first time in your life, you're actually scared that someone will look down on you?"

"I didn't say that," her mother replied defensively.

Sandra clapped her hands together with glee. "You do!" she exclaimed. "You're scared that Harry's going to look down on you! I never thought I'd live to see the day! My mother is *afraid* of someone else! Oh, this is too wonderful!"

"Sandra!" Mrs. Trefontana snapped with enough severity to quiet her, but not to wipe the delighted smile off her face. With an air of affronted dignity she turned back to Harry and said, "I need to ask you one more thing, Harry. You do seem like a very fine young man, and like Sandra said, you are mature beyond your years. And I can see why you two are so smitten with each other, besides the fact that your hormones are racing a hundred miles a minute. You're both shy, timid people, and so you can relate to each other. But Harry, one shy, timid person doesn't need another shy, timid person. They need someone strong to look after them. Sandra's done well for herself, but she still needs someone to look after her. I won't be around forever. Even considering that this May-December arrangement does work out, which I still doubt, what guarantee do I have that you'll be able to look after Sandra, or that she'll be able to look after you? How do I know that you won't both wind up in the gutter?"

This old accusation pierced Harry's heart and bound his tongue. He sat there helplessly.

Sandra put her arms around him. "Mom, you're embarrassing Harry," she pleaded.

"Sandra, this is *my* tête-à-tête with Harry. Shut up. So, Harry, answer my question."

He took a breath, concentrated with all his strength, and managed to say, "I may seem unassuming, Mrs. Trefontana, but I...I can take care of myself. And Sandra can, too. I hope that I can do half as well as she has."

Sandra kissed him. "Good answer," she said.

Mrs. Trefontana sighed. "So you say. But words don't mean anything. What counts are results."

For a moment Harry fell silent again, thinking, *God, please help me.* Then an idea came to him, as if whispered in his ear: *Tell her the joke about the Italian policeman and the Irish policeman.*

"Mrs. Trefontana," Harry said, "what you were saying about the Irish and the Italians—have you ever heard that wonderful old joke about the Italian policeman and the Irish policeman?"

"No, I'm afraid I haven't," she replied.

"Well, I'll tell it to you. I have to warn you, though—this sounds like a joke against the Italians, but it really isn't. You just have to hear it through to the very end."

57

Mrs. Trefontana smiled. "I'm all ears."

"Well, one day, an Irish policeman is walking his beat and he comes upon this little black kid sitting in the gutter, playing with horse dung. And the kid is fashioning it into something, as if he were working with clay. And the Irish cop asks, 'What be ye doing, sonny?' And the kid replies, 'I'm making an Italian policeman.'"

"Harry—" Sandra said nervously.

"Don't worry, honey," he assured her. "You just have to listen to the very end."

"Oh, shut up, Sandra, and let the man finish," Mrs. Trefontana ordered.

"Well, this delights the Irish cop to no end. He runs to the next block and finds an Italian policeman he knows who's walking his beat. 'Top o' the morning to ya, Officer di Georgio,' he says. 'Please come wi' me. I've found something that's verra, verra funny.'

"'And what would-a that be, Officer O'Leary?' asks Officer di Georgio.

"'Never ye mind. Just come wi' me.'

"So Officer di Georgio follows Officer O'Leary back to the next block, and they find the kid still fiddling with the horse dung. 'Sonny,' Officer O'Leary says, 'tell me good friend Officer di Georgio here what ye be doing wi' that horse dung.'

"The kid says, 'I'm making an Italian policeman.'

"Well, Officer di Georgio is outraged. 'What are you-a saying?' he demands. 'How can you-a say you're-a making an Italian policeman out-a horse dung?'

"And the kid says, 'Because I don't have enough shit to make an *Irish* policeman.'"

For a moment there was silence; then pandemonium erupted, as both Sandra and her mother burst into laughter. They doubled over, then straightened up and put their hands to their faces, trying to stifle their laughter; but it was no use, and they collapsed in a fresh round of mirth. Blood congested their features, making their Italian faces seem even darker.

Harry was speechless. He had won.

"Sandra, you stick with this man!" her mother said when she had recovered her voice. "This is a good man! You stick with him, you hear?"

"Oh, darling, you're wonderful, I love you!" Sandra cried, hopping into his lap and covering him with kisses.

"Hey, you kids, stop that!" Mrs. Trefontana said. "This is my house, not a cheap motel!"

"Oh, mom, I love you, too!" Sandra said, and ran over and hugged and kissed her mother furiously.

I did it, Harry thought. It didn't seem possible.

Mrs. Trefontana went over to Harry and took his hands in hers. "Congratulations, Harry," she said. "You passed inspection. Welcome to the family."

"Uh...I did?" he stammered.

"Yes, you silly ass!" She gave him a crushing hug. *Thank you, God*, Harry remembered to think in the midst of his bewilderment. Yet another person had opened her arms and heart to him. Was that possible? Was there that much love in the world?

"Now, let's have dinner," the matriarch ordered.

CHAPTER ELEVEN

"Black people have it easy," Richard said.

"How's that?" Harry asked, puzzled that someone as educated as Richard would make such a statement.

"I mean they can get away with so much that white people can't," he explained. "They can act like such utter shits, and they know that no one will stop them because if they do, they'll be accused of racism."

Harry frowned. "Well, I know that's true in some instances, Richard, but you can't generalize about people like that."

"Oh, cut the humanitarian bullshit, Harry. You're a Republican. Stop trying to sound like a Democrat."

"What's my party affiliation got to do with anything?" Harry asked, his impatience rising. "I was just saying—"

"I know, I know. You can't generalize about people, you can't be bigoted. Well, you can be bigoted if you've lived long enough and had enough experience dealing with people. I wasn't prejudiced, either. Hell, I used to work in the civil rights movement when I was in high school. I marched with my parents in civil rights marches. But after years of teaching black people and living with black people, and seeing how they act, how they think they can get away with things, how they think they're entitled to things because they've suffered so much—well, to hell with them. I'm thoroughly disgusted with them all, even the good ones."

Harry tried to reason with him. "Richard, come on—"

"I've suffered too," he declared, his eyes taking on the weary, blasted look of one who has passed through fire. "I'm pissed off and full of rage, too. I wish to God that I could act it out every day. Then my blood pressure would be under control and I'd be all relaxed, not have any problems. But I can't, because I'm white. I have no 'right' to do that. But they think they *do* have 'rights.' They're 'entitled.' We've all been stepped on and treated like shit, but in the lottery where they decide who gets to take revenge and who doesn't, they won. We lost. So there's nothing to do but sit in the pot and wait for the day when someone will flush you down."

Harry's distaste for what Richard was saying had been replaced by pity for the man; he was so mired in his own hatred and grief that he felt he could do nothing. And the blacks at work did seem to be just as bigoted as Richard was. At least they were amazed that a Republican like himself would treat blacks as if they were fellow human beings. "I can't believe you're a Republican," Frank said on more than one occasion.

"Why shouldn't I be?" Harry asked.

"Well, you seem like such a compassionate person. Compassion and Republicans just don't go together."

"That's ridiculous!" Harry snapped.

"They don't. Come on, Harry. They hate blacks. They hate everybody who isn't rich, white, and thinks like they do. You're just a Republican out of family loyalty, aren't you? Or your rich relatives brainwashed you into thinking that you could be a Republican and not be a bigot."

"Frank, I've told you—"

"I know, I know, they were pissed off about your mama going crazy, so they disinherited the two of you. That don't matter none. You've still been exposed to that outlook. And that's a hard thing to get over. But hey, you've got a good heart—there's hope for you yet."

Denise was better, but she seemed to have a chip on her shoulder as well. One day he was talking to her, and the conversation turned to O. J. Simpson. Harry stated his opinion that the ex-football player had killed his white ex-wife and her white friend.

"I like O. J.," Denise said. "I like what he did to those white people."

Another time, she invited Harry to a party she was giving. He was grateful for the invitation but had to decline, since he and Sandra had tickets for the Folger Shakespeare Company. "There'll be too many black people there for you, huh?" she asked.

"Denise!" he cried. "It's not that!"

She smiled. "Don't worry. I understand. You're just worried that your girlfriend will meet some big handsome black buck there and he'll steal her away. But hey, that's just the way it is. Once you go black, you can't go back. And I know there'll be some cute black girl there to help you get over it."

Harry let out a strangled cry of frustration and left the table.

As for Sally, Harry wondered if the way she acted had anything to do with her being black, and with real or perceived mistreatment that she had suffered. He couldn't tell, and her behavior was so intolerable that he really didn't care.

Of course, the white people at Port Arthur Shoes seemed to have a similar mentality. Richard saw himself as an "entitled" victim of reverse discrimination. Albert was just a snot-nosed kid—Harry felt entitled to call him that, even though Albert was just a year younger than he—but what were snot-nosed kids but young people who felt entitled to irritate older people, because older people were inferior? To Harry's dismay, even Bernice was not immune to the entitlement virus. Once he mentioned to her what Frank had said about Republicans, and she asked incredulously, "You're a Republican? Oh, no!"

He frowned. "Not you, too, Bernice?"

"Well, you're a really nice guy, but gosh, I can't believe that you're a Republican. You seem too open-minded and compassionate."

"I give up," Harry said.

"Well, it's what's in a person's soul that matters, I guess," she mused. "But I just don't have enough money to be a Republican. You don't, either, or you wouldn't be working here."

"Bernice, it—" He sighed. "But don't you think all this talk is…well…just another way of saying, 'I'm entitled, you owe me'?"

"Damned right it is!" she cried. "I've worked hard all my life and gone through so much shit, they *do* owe me something. And they owe you something too, Harry. You put up with all this shit here at work and with trying to get your mother out of the hospital—they owe you something too, you poor guy."

They owe me something… that was the creed at Port Arthur. You could see it in the people's contemptuous glances, in their sour attitude, in their little offensive or wounding actions. This despite the fact that, thanks to Harry, conditions at the store were improving somewhat. Sally had less to complain about, so the employees were happier. And Harry had proven himself a superb problem-solver. Whenever trouble arose—a requested item appeared not to be in stock but probably was, an irritated customer had a complaint, an order or a customer's name had disappeared from the computer files—people called on Harry, and he soon resolved it. Still, the anger and discontent remained percolating just below the surface. That was the way things were in the country as a whole, wasn't it? The economy was booming, people were telling pollsters they were happy with their lives and felt optimistic about the future, but still Americans were angrier than ever, and showing it. Harry prayed for guidance, and hoped that he could rely upon himself to make things better, but the whole affair was sad, and mildly sickening.

What troubled Harry the most was Sally. In the past few weeks, as matters had improved, her attitude toward him had grown positively glacial. When he came to her with the sales figures for the day, she would snap at him, "Leave them on my desk, I ain't got time now." When he came to her with a question, she would say, "I ain't got time," and go back to her work. When he crossed her path in the hall or the break room, she would glare at him as if he were something disgusting; when he asked her a casual question, she would say, "Some of us got work to do around here."

Harry was mortified and bewildered by Sally's behavior, but it did not demolish him as it would have a short while ago. He knew that he was competent, he knew that he was doing a good job, and while this self-knowledge did not shield him from Sally's blows, it did give him the strength to withstand them. Still, he knew that he must figure out how to deal with Sally if matters were truly to improve.

"Don't waste time trying to figure her out," Bernice advised. "She's just mean, and that's all."

Perhaps, Harry thought, but perhaps not. There seemed an air of calculation to everything that Sally did, no matter how spontaneous it seemed. But calculated to do what? What was this evil or sick woman's grand design?

CHAPTER TWELVE

On Saturday, the thirtieth of October, Harry's mother was released from the hospital. Now that the hour had arrived she was terrified of leaving her hated but secure prison and going out into the world again, despite the fact that Sandra had spent every evening of the previous week with her, talking, commiserating, holding her tight. Harry had wanted to spend time with her as well, but Sandra had vetoed the idea; his mother needed someone who understood the pain of crippling illness and its attendant fear. Feeling unutterably sad and impotent, but knowing that Sandra was right, he agreed.

When Harry arrived at the hospital ten minutes before the agreed-upon departure time of 9:00, he felt strangely humble and reticent. This place, secure in its grim solidity, had kept his mother captive for so long: would it let her go without a fight? Was it mightier than all of them, and they had no right to challenge it? He shook these thoughts from his mind; he had to set her free. He took the elevator up to the fourth floor and hurried to his mother's room, where he found his mother wearing her one good dress and sitting on the bed. Sandra sat beside her and held her, whispering encouragement in her ear.

"Hello," said Harry weakly. He could think of nothing else to say.

His mother regarded him with a look of terror. He rushed toward her, but Sandra stopped him with an upraised hand. "Harry, let me handle this," she said.

Feeling that those who had thought him weak and ineffectual had understated the case, Harry stood by and did nothing.

"Sweetheart," Sandra told Mrs. McCreedy, "you don't want to die in this place, do you? You want to die surrounded by people who love you and would do anything for you. You want to live out your life with your family. We're your family, Harry and I, and we want to be with you. This place is a prison. Our apartment is a place of love and joy and peace, a place where you'll be free, and yet it's so secure, as secure as a padded cell. Darling,

God wants you to be with us. He wants you to be free. He wants you to be loved. We're here to set you free. Trust me, the ride to the apartment will only take a few minutes. Imagine, just a few minutes and then you'll be in the place you've always wanted to be! Won't that be wonderful?"

Harry's mother dropped her head, and tears began to roll down her face. "I'm so sorry," she whispered. "I'm acting like such a ninny."

"Now stop that!" Sandra cried. "You're not to put yourself down. You're the most wonderful person in the world, so start acting like you know you are!"

Mrs. McCreedy moaned and leaned against Sandra's breast. Sandra held her there for a long time, letting her sob her heart out. Finally, the older woman raised her head and said, "I—I'm ready to go now."

"Good," Sandra said. Harry, who had been watching this scene with ever-tightening nerves, let out an audible gasp of relief. "Come on, mother, I'll get your suitcase," he said, and did so, then joined Sandra in helping his mother rise to her feet. They moved to the door slowly but did not falter; then they passed through it, then they were moving down the hall, then they were taking the elevator down to the first floor, then they were negotiating the long corridor leading to the front door of the hospital. At last they were through it, and creeping toward Harry's car; then, finally, they were inside the car, with his mother securely stowed between Sandra and himself in the front seat.

Mrs. McCreedy covered her face. "The sun hurts my eyes," she said.

"No problem," Sandra replied and, taking a pair of dark glasses from her purse, put them on Mrs. McCreedy.

"That's much better," the older woman whispered. "Thank you."

Sandra kissed her, then Harry, feeling very gallant, asked, "Shall we?"

"Yes, hurry, hurry," Sandra said.

Harry started up the car, and pulled it out of the parking lot as fast as he reasonably could; then they were driving down the street, and his mother began to tremble. Sandra took a small pouch from her purse, then pulled a rosary out of it and placed it in one of Mrs. McCreedy's hands. "I got this for you," Sandra told her. "It will comfort you."

Tears came to Harry's mother's eyes as she looked at Sandra, then back at her new rosary. She raised it to her mouth and kissed the crucifix, then began to work the beads between her feeble, trembling fingers. Sandra took her in her arms and began to rock her, as if she were a child.

Watching this, Harry felt a stabbing, tingling sensation in his chest. He had promised himself that he would not cry, but the sensation rose in his throat and spread to his eyes, making tears flow. He wiped them away and tried to steel himself. A loving hand was laid on his shoulder; he turned and looked. It was Sandra, who mouthed the words "I love you" to him.

Soon they reached Sandra's apartment building. The previous week, they had reached a decision: Mrs. McCreedy would stay in Sandra's apartment, since it was much bigger than Harry's. And, since there was room for three there, Harry would move in as well, thus eliminating the silly pretense that he and Sandra lived separate lives. His insurance and savings would cover his mother's medical expenses; he and Sandra would share the rent evenly, thereby saving him a couple hundred dollars per month.

"Come on, darling," Sandra coaxed as she opened the passenger's-side door. "We're here. Just a minute longer, and you'll be safe."

Mrs. McCreedy paused, kissed the crucifix of the rosary again, then slowly, steadily inched her way out of the car. Once outside she paused for a moment, and seemed in danger of collapsing, but Harry and Sandra held her up, and she regained her strength. They made it through the door, and across the relatively small but seemingly interminable main lobby; then they were at the elevator, the doors opened, and they stepped inside and rode to the third floor. The doors opened again, and Mrs. McCreedy again paused; but Sandra urged her on with, "Come on, darling, hurry, we're almost there." They fairly slid down the hall to the door of Sandra's apartment. Harry quickly unlocked the door, and Sandra gently guided and pushed his mother into the apartment.

Once inside, Mrs. McCreedy's manner changed. She removed the glasses and looked round in wide-eyed, open-mouthed amazement, like an explorer first beholding a wonder of the earth. Sandra and Harry huddled round her, waiting for her next reaction; then, finally, her gaze settled upon them. "I am here," she said with childlike wonder.

"Yes, you are, mother," Harry said. This realization filled his mind, making him giddy. His mother was here! And safe. The edicts of the world's cruel justice had been overthrown; she was out in the world again, and as Sandra said, surrounded by love. Weakness did not have to be punished by endless suffering and a cruel, lonely death. His body and mind, freed suddenly from the strain of years of hoping and praying and working for this moment, nearly collapsed.

Then an astonishing thing happened: Mrs. McCreedy, filled for an instant with a healthy person's strength, reached out and grabbed both Harry and Sandra, and pulled them to her. She took in a deep, healthy person's breath, then let it out as if she had many more to spare. "I *am* safe," she said. "Thank you."

From then on, Harry, his mother, and Sandra lived together as one family. And a curious transformation took place: Harry, reunited with his mother after over a decade, somehow lost her. She was Sandra's mother now, for all intents and purposes, and Sandra was her daughter. Harry took care of his mother's food and medication and medical bills, but it was Sandra who cooked her food, made certain that she took her medicine on time, and fussed over her with a hearty protectiveness that made Harry love Sandra all the more. He did not mourn his loss, or begrudge Sandra her gain. His mother had passed from Hell to an earthly Paradise, and that was all that mattered.

As if to compensate for this unmourned loss, Harry found himself spending more time with Sandra's mother. The woman was quite taken with him, but still suffered lingering doubts about his ability to handle the world and to provide for her daughter;

hence her frequent and not unpleasant inquisitions of him. During one of these inquisitions, in the middle of November, Harry made the decision that would end his life.

CHAPTER THIRTEEN

On Tuesday, 16 November, Harry was sitting in his small cubbyhole of an office lost in contemplation—or, rather, in an attempt at contemplation. Nothing came of his efforts, for his mind simply did not want to think of the terrible and puzzling thing that had just taken place; its audacity took his breath away. Then, to his surprise, Sandra's mother peeked through the open door of his office.

"Hello, there," she said with an impish grin. "What are you up to?"

"Mrs. Trefontana," Harry said. "What a surprise." He rose from his chair.

"I wanted to see where you worked and watch you in action a little, so I decided to pop in unannounced."

"That's quite all right. Have a seat." She did so, and he asked, "So, what do you think of the place?"

"Big," she replied. "A pretty impressive place."

"Thank you. I think so, too. It's so big, and I always have to be walking somewhere or other, so it's a very open place to work in…it sort of makes you feel like you're out in the wide open spaces."

"That was a very poetic statement," Mrs. Trefontana remarked. "You're a very sensitive man, Harry. A man of deep feelings."

"Well, thank you," he said.

"But you weren't walking around just now. You were sitting her looking very troubled. What's wrong?"

He paused and sighed. "Well, something terrible happened this morning, Mrs. Trefontana. It was—I still can't believe it."

"What was it? Tell me about it. You'll feel better."

"Well, I'm not certain that's true," he said, "but I'll tell you."

Early that morning, shortly after the store opened for business, Sally asked to see Harry in her office. Harry was puzzled, given Sally's recent attitude toward him. Was she, he wondered anxiously, going to fire him? But somehow he knew that she would not do that. This must be about something else. He hurried to her office.

"Close the door and sit down," she said when he entered. She spoke, Harry noted with relief, in a pleasant, almost musical voice.

He followed her orders, and she leaned back in her chair and said, "Harry, first of all, I'd like to say that you're doing a great job here."

"Why...thank you, Sally," he said, his pleasure at this remark momentarily overcoming his suspicion.

"And I think that you're going to go really far here, or whatever place you end up at. I'm sorry I've been such a bitch the last few weeks, but I had to see if you were worthy of my respect first. This is a hard world, you know. You got to toughen people up so they can fight their own battles. When you first came here, you seemed awful weak, and I didn't think that you could make it. Well, I guess I was wrong, and I don't mind admitting that."

"Thank you," Harry said grimly, his happiness replaced by an anger that he could scarcely conceal.

"Which is why I wanted to talk to you now." She leaned forward across her desk. "I'm up for a promotion next fall, after they do our next performance reviews. I might be getting myself an executive position. And you know what that would mean for you, don't you? You'd get my job, probably."

Harry started. He had not dreamed of being promoted so rapidly. When no reply from him was forthcoming, Sally went on, "But none of that's gonna happen unless we work together."

"What do you mean?" he asked.

"I mean, you're doing your job *too* well. Morale's starting to improve around here—not much, but it was so bad before that any little improvement seems like a lot. And that makes me look bad. It makes it look like I was fucking things up around here, and then you came along and saved the day. That makes me look bad, don't you see?"

Harry listened in shocked silence. He could not believe

this, it was impossible. Human beings, he knew well, were capable of the most devious and diabolical schemes, but they kept those schemes to themselves. Never, outside of the theater, did they admit them to others, or take such outward pride in them.

"So here's what I want you to do," Sally said. "I want you to keep coming up with little technical suggestions to make things run smoother around here, like you been doing. But I don't want you to get too close to the other people around here, make them think that you're their friend, or give them hope that things will get better. If they do, then I'll get fired, don't you see? When my performance review comes up next, I want to be able to say, 'Look, I've done a good job managing these people as far as their sales records go, but I ain't been able to do nothing with them personally. Do you see what shit I've had to put up with, and how I've done so much good in spite of them?' That way they'll think I'm some hot shit manager, plus they'll want to reward me for having put up with all this shit for so long. Don't you see? It's the only way I'll get ahead around here, and I didn't take this job so I could fall behind."

Harry could not speak; his expression was one of horrified bewilderment.

"So when that happens, I'll get a promotion, and so will you, and all these fucking idiots will get fired, and we can hire a whole new batch of better people," Sally said. "Don't you see? Don't you think that's a good plan?"

Still he could not speak.

"Do you or don't you?" she asked, a tone of her old menace beginning to creep into her voice. "Answer me!"

He opened his mouth to do so, but his voice was locked away.

She regarded him with a hard, cold stare for a moment; then she extended her right index finger, and the long fingernail at its end, toward him. "Well, you better do what I say, or I'll fuck up your life so bad you'll wish that you hadn't been born. Do you hear me?"

Finally he managed to nod.

"Now get on out," she said. "I got work to do."

Like a zombie, he rose and left her office.

"What a bitch," Mrs. Trefontana remarked when Harry had finished. "What an absolute bitch."

"That is an understatement," Harry replied.

"So what are you going to do about it?" she demanded. "You're not going to go along with her game and ruin these other people's lives, are you?"

"No, of course not. But I don't know what else I'm going to do."

She frowned. "Harry, I thought that you had spunk. I thought that you had guts underneath that shy exterior. You're not going to be a wet noodle, are you?"

"No, ma'am, I'm not, but…this is so strange. How on earth can you deal with someone who's so…wicked, and proud of it?"

"By attacking her head on," she declared. "The same thing you have to do with the devil, the world, and life in general. Otherwise you'll be plowed under."

"That's obvious. But how?"

"Well, can't you tell whoever runs this company about it?" He sighed. "I've already tried that."

Her eyes raised in surprise. "You have?"

"Yes, I called him this morning and asked if I could speak with him. He asked me what it was about. I said I had a problem with one of my colleagues, a problem of ethics, and he told me to.get it in writing and give it to him when performance reviews are due."

"But that's almost a year away!"

"Exactly. Mr. Eldridge—that's the company president— doesn't really like to be confronted with unpleasant things, I've heard, and now I believe it. If you want my honest opinion, I don't think he's done a very good job managing the company. I looked up some more about our company's rating in the literature, and it's really declined since he took over. Before that, we were expanding like there was no tomorrow, but since he came on board, growth has stagnated."

"I wonder why," Mrs. Trefontana quipped.

"Fortunately, he's planning on retiring at the end of next

year. The vice-president, David Eadel, is another story. From what I've read and heard, he's very highly thought of—he'll put us back on the right track. Unfortunately, he won't be taking over until the end of next year, so I'll have to deal with Eldridge on the matter of Sally. That's not good. Not good at all."

"You're going to keep a written record of this, aren't you?" she asked.

"I don't see what else I can do."

"That won't be enough," she declared. "That hard-headed son of a bitch isn't going to pay attention to just one man's statement. You say that this bitch Sally is always giving everyone around here a hard time, insulting them and treating them like shit?"

"That's a very accurate way of putting it."

"Well, then, you're going to have to get everyone around here to keep a record of how she treats them, too. You're going to have to get everyone to write it down whenever this bitch does something awful. That way, this man will have a mountain of evidence facing him, and he'll have to act. My late husband, may he rest in peace, once handled a lawsuit brought by a group of employees against their employer, and he was almost as bad as Sally is. My husband told them that, when they brought the lawsuit into court, they'd have to have written evidence of all the bad things their employer had done to them. So all of them started keeping journals, and when they went into court, they had all this evidence to back up their suit, and they won the case. And that's what you're going to have to do."

"That's a wonderful idea," Harry said. "But I don't know if everyone else will go along with it."

"Well, then you'll just have to *make* them go along with it," she declared. "Harry, this is life and death here—or job and no job, rather. If they won't go along with you, then you'll just have to *make* them get up off their asses and go along. Harry, I...I'm worried about Sandra. I've got to know that she'll be well taken care of when I'm gone."

"Mrs. Trefontana," Harry said firmly but with sympathy, "I really think that you underestimate Sandra. She's an incredibly strong person. She can look after herself."

"No, she can't," the mother declared. "Maybe right now she can, but sometime, when another big crisis comes along, she'll fold up like an accordion, just like she did before. And I want her to have someone strong to look after her. I thought that you were a strong person underneath, or that you might be one eventually. Please don't let me find out that I was wrong."

She looked at him sternly, and for an instant he wilted beneath her gaze; but he wanted to protect Sandra too, even if she didn't need protecting, so he marshaled himself and replied, in a firm strong voice, "All right, Mrs. Trefontana. That's an excellent idea, and I'll try it out. I'll ask the others about it."

A bright, toothy smile—an exact replica of Sandra's—spread across her face. "Good boy," she said. She got up and walked over to Harry and put her hands on his shoulders. "You're a very fine young man, Harry, which is why I've decided to ignore the huge question of the age difference between you and Sandra. I might forget it forever if you show me that you've got what our Hispanic brothers and sisters in the Faith call *cojones*."

He chuckled. "I'll try, Mrs. Trefontana, I'll try. But one thing. How am I going to do all this and still not make it seem that I'm too friendly with my coworkers? I'm going to have to seem to be keeping a little distance from them, to get Sally off my back."

She tousled his hair. "Well, you're a smart boy—think of something! I'm not here to do your thinking for you—not all of it, anyway."

CHAPTER FOURTEEN

The next day, Harry invited each of his coworkers to a meeting at his apartment the following evening, cautioning them to say nothing about it to Sally or anyone else. He had, he told them, thought of a way to rid the place of Sally once and for all.

Except for Albert, who claimed a prior engagement—"My evenings are reserved for doing nothing," he said—everyone agreed to come. At the appointed time, Sandra took Harry's mother out for a walk around Georgetown. By ten minutes after seven, his coworkers had arrived and seated themselves in the living room. Nervously but with determination, Harry rose and began to speak.

"I asked you to come here—and I appreciate your taking the time. I know you've all got families or your own private lives to deal with—to help deal with a very serious problem. We're all unhappy with the environment at work. And I think we all agree that Sally is a large part of the problem. She's—well, she's Sally!" He tried to laugh, but it came out as a nervous giggle.

"She's a fucking bitch," Richard said.

"Richard, as always, said it best," Harry went on. "If we want things to improve at Port Arthur, we've got to get rid of the Sally problem. Ordinarily, in a situation like this, you'd want to try and talk things over with the person first, try and help them to see the error of their ways and give them a chance to change. I think we all agree that, in Sally's case, that's like hoping the moon will suddenly turn out to be made of green cheese."

There was general agreement.

"But, until the day before yesterday, I didn't realize just how far from being able to reform herself Sally is, and how hard dealing with the Sally problem is going to be." He told them what had happened, and by the time he finished, the others' faces had become distorted with shock, rage, and disgust.

Frank shot to his feet. "I'll kill her!" he screamed, spraying spit all over the coffee table. "I'll kill her! I'll kill that fucking bitch!"

Harry ran over and took hold of him. "Frank!" he cried. "Calm down!"

"I'll kill her! I'll fucking kill her!"

"Frank!" Denise's voice rang out. "Sit down, and *shut up!*"

Suddenly Frank's rage ceased, and he looked at Harry like a frightened child. "We got to get her," he said quietly. "We got to stop her."

"And we will," Harry replied. "Now sit down." Frank did so.

"Now then," Harry continued, "we have two options. Either we can do nothing, or we can keep records of what Sally does so that we can use them against her when the performance reviews come up. I'd like to claim that idea as my own, but it's not. It was Sandra's mother's idea. Well, I am one man who's not afraid when a woman has a good idea. And I think that we should all follow that dear lady's suggestion. I'm certainly going to, and the more of you who agree to do the same, the more ammunition we'll have to use against her. So what do you say?"

"I'm with you," Richard said.

"Me, too," Denise chimed in.

"Making her get her comeuppance will be better than sex," Bernice added.

"We got to nail her," Frank said. "We got to nail her good."

"That's what we're trying to do, Frank," Harry reminded him.

"Yeah, but we got to do more than that. We got to plant her ass six feet under the ground. We got to do what my mama did with that woman who said that some of us really were niggers."

Harry winced at the thought of what Frank's mother had done. "I don't think we need go that far, Frank."

"Why not? She's dissing us. We're children of God, and she's spitting in God's Face when she's dissing us. Now what's God going to say on Judgment Day about us not standing up for Him?"

"Sally's a child of God too, Frank, no matter how badly she acts." That was the truth, but his own words made Harry wince; they sounded so sanctimonious.

"No, she's not. She's a child of the devil. There's nothing in the Scriptures that says you have to be good to children of the devil."

"But, Frank—oh, forget it. So you're all with me?"

Everyone was.

"That's great. So you'll all keep regular, accurate records of every bad, rude, or unprofessional thing that Sally does—in short, you'll record her every word and deed?"

They promised they would.

A feeling of triumph surged in Harry's breast. Once again the world seemed capable of being mastered; he was, truly, a man in charge.

"There's one other thing," he said. "I'm certainly not going to forget my responsibilities as an assistant manager—Bernice isn't, either—but I'm going to have to give you guys a little more autonomy, because if things keep on getting better and Sally sees me trying to manage you guys all the time, then the game is up. Of course, she wants me to do nothing and for you guys to act the way you did before—but I hope we all agree that that's not an option."

"I wouldn't give the bitch the satisfaction," Richard said, and everyone seconded this.

"That's good. So we're going to keep on getting better and better, and we're all going to improve—but each on his or her own initiative, not so much as a group effort. Sally will be very angry, but she won't be able to blame it on me, or on us as a whole. Are we agreed?"

Everyone was, except for Frank. "This is too passive," he said. "We're attacking her with pens and paper when we need to slice her with a box cutter, like my mama would have done."

Harry's patience snapped. "Frank, our pens and paper *are* box cutters. We're going to slice her with them so much there won't be a square inch of her left." He stopped, horrified by his words, and by the violence that had come out of him as easily as his expelled breath.

"Yeah!" Denise agreed. "Listen to him!"

"Well, I think we all agree that we've got to get rid of Sally," Harry said weakly. "And that's what we're going to do."

He felt sick inside. Other people's violence had infected his soul to the point that he was starting to think like them. And he was encouraging them to persist in their violent attitudes! But what else could he do? Sally must be stopped. So he would help his coworkers to stoke the fires of their hatred of Sally, and to turn those fires upon her. He hoped that it would be a purifying blaze, and would not singe too many hairs on others' heads.

CHAPTER FIFTEEN

The following day, Harry wrote up an account of his conversation with Sally. As he was printing it out, Sally came into his office to tell him about a meeting scheduled for that afternoon. Harry's heart stopped, he broke out in a cold sweat; but fortunately Sally showed no interest in what he was doing, and left quickly. *From now on, I'm writing these reports at home,* he told himself.

His coworkers, except for Albert, began to keep journals detailing Sally's bad behavior, and showed their journal entries to Harry. He thought them very concise and thorough, and was freshly amazed and disgusted at just how far off the scale of basic decency Sally had gone.

"I went to Sally to ask her when a new line of shoes would be coming out," Denise wrote in a typical entry. "She accused me of being lazy and told me to look it up on the Internet, like everyone else. I told her that I was busy with customers all day and didn't have time to look things up on the Internet during work hours, but she told me not to make excuses and get out."

"Sally came to me today," Richard wrote in his journal, "and asked me why my rate of sales for the past week was down five percent from the week before. I told her that I honestly didn't know, that sales figures naturally fluctuated from week to week, and that the difference wasn't a cause for concern. Then she got terribly angry with me and said that this was the kind of attitude that was ruining the American work ethic, and that while white people usually accused black people like her of being lazy, that they were the ones who were really lazy. She went on in this vein for over five minutes."

Bernice wrote, "Sally kept asking me why I hadn't thought up the ideas that Harry did—revising our sales records and the computer program that tabulated them. I said that I guessed that Harry was just smarter than me. Sally replied, 'If you think you're too dumb for this job, then why don't you just quit?' and smiled and walked away."

Frank wrote, "Sally asked me today why I hadn't gotten pissed off at Albert lately. I said that Albert had been behaving himself lately, and also that I'd decided to take more of a 'live and let live' attitude. She asked, 'Did Harry tell you to do that?' I said, 'No, I came to that decision myself.' She called me a liar, and I started to get angry, but I caught myself in time, and she commented on that: 'Why don't you get pissed off at me?' I asked her, 'Do you want me to get pissed off at you?' And she said, 'Yeah! It's good for a laugh.' And then she walked away."

Of all these entries, it was an entry in Harry's own journal that saddened him most. "I went to give Sally the week's sales figures," he wrote on the second of December, "but all she was interested in was whether or not anybody's sales figures were down. She was very disappointed when I told her that they were not. Then she asked me, 'Couldn't we—lower a couple of them?' I was flabbergasted and asked her what she meant. She asked, 'What do you think I mean? I mean that if we change the figures, then some of those fools will start looking bad, and they'll get fired.' I had promised myself that I wouldn't let her intimidate me or disconcert me ever again, but I couldn't help it; I was just dumbfounded that she would make a suggestion like that. Thankfully, when she saw that I wasn't keen on the idea, she dismissed it by saying, 'Well, it was just an idea.' But it wasn't."

As the weeks passed and the Christmas holidays approached, the pile of written evidence began to grow page by page. For now it was only a small mound over which a person might trip, but before long it would be a mountain that would bar the way of even the most intrepid. The process of solving "the Sally problem" had begun; when Eldridge found out just how bad Sally was, he would have to act.

CHAPTER SIXTEEN

On 18 December, the Saturday before Christmas, Harry was awakened, as he was every morning, by Sandra crawling out of bed to check on his mother. He had nearly fallen asleep again when she returned, removed her nightgown, and crawled back into bed. "She's fine," Sandra reported. "She didn't have any angina attacks last night. She looked so cute sitting there on the sofa eating cereal and reading the paper. She just looked so happy. And after she took her medicine she insisted I go back to bed. She said, 'You kids work so hard, you need your rest, and your— well—you know.'" She laughed and lay across Harry's chest. Her dark brown hair fell onto his chest; the warmth of her body seeped into his; her natural smell, mingled with the odors of last night's lovemaking, filled his nostrils; her nurturing attitude made him feel safe. Within a minute, they were inside each other. Later, toward the end, while he struggled through the last stretch of work needed to reach bliss, Harry looked down and saw Sandra's face congested with passion, and thought it the most beautiful sight he had ever seen. "Sandra," he grunted, "will you marry me?"

"Oh, yes," she gasped. "Yes—yes—yes—yes," she repeated, in rhythm with their mutual thrusting.

"Shall we give my priest notice right away—and then get married—in the summer?" he asked, his grunts resolving themselves into a long, low moan.

"Today—we'll call him—today," she spat out, her breath coming faster and more ragged.

He managed to say, "I love you," then could no longer speak. The struggle was over, and they had won their prize. They thrust their tongues into each other's mouths to stifle their cries, the vibrations of which flowed, like their juices, from one of them to the other.

They slept for another hour, then got up to have breakfast and tell his mother the news. "I knew it was coming," she said with a beatific smile. "I'm so happy. This is the happiest day of my life."

When they visited Mrs. Trefontana that afternoon to tell her the news, she reacted far more volubly. "Oh, my baby!" she said, and imprisoned Sandra in a crushing hug. "Oh, my baby! I'm so happy! You're going to have a good life and someone to look after you! Oh, my baby, my baby, my baby." She gave Sandra one bruising kiss after another.

When she finally let Sandra go, she turned to Harry. "So you're convinced?" he asked nervously. "You think that I can take care of Sandra?"

She smiled. "Harry, I'm sure of it."

"And the age difference? It—"

She clamped her hand over his mouth. "That topic is never to be discussed again."

"Then I won?" Harry asked with childlike hope.

"Yes, you did." She held him tight. "Oh, Harry, my son, my son, my son. I never thought I'd have a son."

"Well—" Harry began, but he could not speak, so he just let her hold him. After a moment, he found his voice. "Am I really your son now?"

She messed up his hair. "As if you were my very own."

CHAPTER SEVENTEEN

The Christmas season—always Harry's favorite time of year, though for the past dozen years he had been unable to enjoy it fully, and sometimes not at all—passed in a merry, beneficent haze. He and Sandra and his mother spent Christmas at Mrs. Trefontana's house, and it was a blessed event, with presents and games and quiet time spent together and Mass with Gregorian chants at Old St. Mary's and (after the parents had gone to bed) a long night of making love before the Christmas fire. Harry and Sandra had been worried that his mother would find the required jollity of Christmas an impossible burden, and would run and hide in a closet, but she did not. "This was the happiest Christmas of my life," she told Harry and Sandra as they tucked her into bed on the night of the twenty-fifth.

The following week came New Year's Eve, the beginning of the last year of the old millennium, and the four of them went to the Lincoln Memorial for the Capitol's multimedia celebration. It was exhilarating, despite the participation of President Clinton. Then, sadly, the holidays were over, and "real life" ruled their lives once more. At Port Arthur, however, things were very different.

For one thing, Sally was actually being nice to people. She had always been able to put on a show of niceness when her interests demanded it, but now she was positively drowning everyone in a sickening display of sweetness. No one was fooled by her act, but they suffered her newfound interest in every detail of their lives. Harry did so too, until one time when he sat in the break room eating his lunch and overheard Sally and Denise discussing the pitfalls of fellatio.

"It may make men feel real good," Denise said, "but I don't like to have that thing in my mouth. You pee out of that."

"I don't mind that," Sally replied, "but I don't like to swallow that stuff. It tastes real bad."

"Ladies, please!" Harry cried. "I'm trying to eat my lunch, and you're making me sick!"

"Ooooh, he's all offended," Sally mocked. "Ain't he the virtuous one. I'll bet he makes his fiancee do that to him all the time."

"Yeah, old Harry's a wild guy under that expensive suit," Denise said, winking at him.

"Yeah," Sally went on, "I'll bet you got that girl—what's her name?"

"Sandra," he replied.

"I'll bet you got her jaws working overtime. I'll bet you make her swallow so much of your cum that she don't even need to drink water. You do that, don't you?"

Harry was so offended that he actually snapped, "None of your business!"

"Ooooh, he's offended," Sally mocked. "That means he does do it."

Denise came partly to his rescue. "Oh, Harry likes to give pleasure too. And I'll bet he makes Sandra real happy. Don't you, Harry?"

For some reason—being beaten down by this assault, perhaps, or the need to assert his manhood—Harry replied, "Well, that's what she says."

That evening, as they lay in bed, Harry told Sandra what had happened that day. He didn't want to admit that he had finally responded to their goading, but he believed in honesty, and so, burning with shame and with many groveling apologies, he did so.

"Those people are pigs," Sandra declared. "Harry, I'm so sorry that you have to work with people like that. It's beneath you. Everyone at that place just sounds like an utter pig."

"Only sometimes," he replied. "And I'm trying to make things better around there."

She paused before asking, "Harry—would you rather work somewhere else?"

"Oh, no, no!" he almost shouted. "I have a promise that I have to keep."

"I know, and you're an honorable man, Harry, but—is it worth enduring all that stuff just to keep your promise? I'm worried that you're hurting yourself. You have responsibilities to yourself, too. You deserve to be happy, to be treated with respect. There are plenty of much better jobs that you could get—in sales, with corporations, with the government. I could really help you if you wanted to get a government job."

Sandra was playing her nurturing role, and Harry loved it. It was *wonderful* being nurtured, especially if you had endured more than a decade without much nurturing. He pulled Sandra to him. "I love you so much," he said. "But Sandra, I promised that I'd try to change things around there. And things are changing for the better—if we get rid of Sally, perhaps they'll change permanently. I promised I'd do something, and it's yielding fruit. I can't leave now. I don't want to work at Port Arthur the rest of my life, but I have to stay there for now. Besides, I may get a promotion and lots of good references out of this, if I succeed in changing things. If I left now, I'd be hurting myself. And besides…if I left now, it would be like cutting out some vital organ. Things would never be the same."

"You are so good," she said reverently. "Harry, promise me that you'll always be good and that you'll always show me how people are supposed to live. Do you promise me that?"

"I'll try," he said.

"Good." She rolled him over onto his back and began to kiss, bite, and rub her way down his chest. "Now, if you'll excuse me, I've got to exercise my jaws."

"Oh, stop it!" Harry said, trying to stifle his laughter.

"I'm very thirsty," she went on, "and I never drink water or any other liquids, so I need a nice, hot drink to keep me going…"

"Will you *stop* it!" Harry laughed, kicking her away with his knees.

She pinned him down and got to work.

CHAPTER EIGHTEEN

Harry's grandfather had long wanted to visit him and see how Harry's foolish but brave attempt to walk in his father's footsteps was going. Harry, terrified of the old gentleman's disapproval, held him off for as long as possible, but finally gave in and arranged for his grandfather to visit him at Port Arthur on 11 February, the Friday before Valentine's Day.

Harry waited outside the store for his grandfather, trying hard to look both distinguished and casual. Thank heaven the old man was in the city on business and was thus staying at a hotel; ordinarily he would have wanted to stay with Sandra and he, but of course he would not suffer to be in the same room with Harry's mother. Besides, Sandra had refused to meet with any of his father's family, except at the wedding, unless they started treating his mother with respect.

His grandfather came walking up, as always dressed in a gray three-piece pinstriped suit, wearing a matching gray hat, and carrying a cane. "Harry, my boy," he said in his elegant Back Bay accent. "Good to see you again."

"Good to see you again, sir," Harry said. They shook hands. "Shall we go inside?"

"By all means."

They entered the show room. "Very impressive place," his grandfather remarked.

"Isn't it?" Harry said. "I'll see if any of my coworkers are free—" He looked round, but only Frank and Denise were on the floor, and they were busy with customers. *Oh, God,* Harry realized. *He'll think this is a low-class place because so many black people work here.* Then he reproached himself: *What's wrong with you? Why are you thinking like this? Don't get in the gutter to earn another person's respect; it's not worth it!* "Perhaps they're in the break room," he said. "Come on, grandfather."

As they walked to the break room, his grandfather asked, "When are your performance reviews coming up, Harry?"

"In the fall, grandfather."

"Well, you're doing well, unless what you told me was a pack of lies. And you're a truthful person, even if your head isn't always in the right place. Perhaps you'll get a promotion."

"I certainly hope so."

They reached the break room, but no one was there. "Do you want some coffee, grandfather?" he asked.

"Yes, please."

He poured both of them some coffee, then asked, "Would you like to go to my office?"

"Absolutely."

They went there and sat down. His grandfather noted the framed images of Our Lady of Guadalupe and Our Mother of Perpetual Help hanging on the walls and remarked, "You still haven't lost your faith, I see, Harry."

"No, sir. I don't think I could keep breathing without it."

"Good, good. When a man goes out into the world and becomes preoccupied with worldly cares, too often he loses sight of his faith. That's always a great danger."

"Well, not for me, sir."

"Good. And that picture on your desk—is that Sandra?"

"Yes, sir." He handed the picture to his grandfather, who appraised it closely and judged, "Very beautiful. Of course, she is a lot older than you, Harry, but from what you say, she's from a good family and has done very well for herself. She's Italian, I assume?"

"Uh...yes," Harry admitted nervously.

"Well, we'll let that pass. So, when is the wedding going to be?"

"June the twenty-fourth."

"And it will be held where?"

"At Old St. Mary's, where Sandra and I go. We were hoping to reserve the Crypt Church at the Basilica, but it's already booked solid for the summer."

"Well, weddings shouldn't be too ostentatious." Then the old gentleman's eyes fell upon a picture of Harry's mother, and his pale blue eyes went hard with anger. As fast as a lizard sticks out its tongue, Harry reached out and turned the picture face down.

"Thank you," his grandfather said, and continued in his former pleasant air, "So, you wanted to experience life the way the family has always lived it. What do you think of it now?"

Harry sighed. "Very challenging, sir, but...worth the effort."

The old man eyed him shrewdly. "Not too challenging, is it?"

"Oh, no, sir."

"But it's not exactly a bed of roses, is it?"

"Oh, of course not, but then I never expected it to be." He tried to steel himself; his grandfather was scrutinizing him closely for any sign of weakness.

"What are the problems this job presents to you, Harry?"

Harry paused. He knew that he must be honest, but the problems that he faced here were surely much nastier, much more brutal and low-class, than any that his grandfather had ever had to face in the business world. They cried out, "This is a low-class place!" and, while Harry did not ordinarily think in terms of class or race, his grandfather did, and he wanted his grandfather's approval—or at least dreaded his criticism.

But there was nothing to do but tell the truth. Calmly, and with a tone of resigned despair, he told his grandfather everything. When he had finished, the old man, to Harry's great surprise, chuckled.

"Oh, dear, oh, dear," he said, "human nature is so petty and so dreadfully predictable. Nothing that's happening here is at all uncommon, or even surprising, if you've spent any time out in the world. I hope that makes you feel a little better, Harry. You seem to think that what's going on here is all some frightful aberration, but I assure you it's not."

"Really?" Harry asked, astonished.

The old man laughed. "You're still as naïve as you've always been, aren't you? Harry, the world is a jungle. The people who survive are not necessarily the biggest or the strongest or the most brutal, but those who know how to navigate the dangers of the jungle. Oh, if you're cornered, then you have to fight, and fight with all your strength, and then it's a victory fairly won. But most of the time, one simply has to know how to get through the maze of life, knowing where to go and what dangers and traps to avoid. That's the key to success in life, whether you're a lavatory attendant or the most powerful man in the world. You must learn that if you want to survive. Your father knew that—knew it better than I or anyone else I've ever known—but circumstances beyond his control took him out of the game entirely, poor boy."

There was silence, as both men coped with the weight of their loss. Harry's grandfather recovered first, and said, "But Harry, you are making an effort to learn all this. That's something, a great deal, in fact. Let's just say that the role of a crafty navigator isn't one that comes entirely naturally to you. If it came naturally to you, as it did to your father and, I dare say, to myself, then it wouldn't mean much, really."

Harry couldn't believe his ears. Was his grandfather actually saying that he had accomplished *more* than the other McCreedys had?

"I'd like to meet your future bride," the old man said.

Harry winced.

"What is it, my boy?" his grandfather asked.

Harry swallowed. "Well...Sandra has really fallen in love—there's no better phrase for it—with my mother. She's really taken over the role of my mother's caretaker and absolutely adores her. And she—well—she's angry about how you and the rest of the family—feel about her. And she refuses to see you unless you meet with my mother again and...treat her better."

"Ah, so she's a sentimentalist, like you," his grandfather said. "Now I understand the secret of your attraction. But she does sound like a girl of spirit. Well then, Harry, I suppose a meeting now is out of the question. But perhaps sometime in the future. I mean, I am invited to your wedding, aren't I?"

"Well, of course, grandfather."

"Then at that time, if not before." The old man paused and looked thoughtful. "Harry, you doubtless think that I and the rest of the family are hypocrites, don't you, for upholding the Faith but not speaking to your mother, don't you?"

Harry's silence provided the answer.

"Well, you young people are quick to judge, especially if you're judging your elders. You shouldn't be. Life has a very strange way of entangling you in its uglier aspects, like vines entangling a tree. And before long—perhaps from the beginning—you come to enjoy, or at least to depend upon, those unsavory things so much that they end up taking possession of you. That's not an excuse—we are all ultimately responsible for what we do, the devil may tempt us, but we can always say no—but it is the truth. You haven't been immune from temptation either, you know—you're living in sin with Sandra when you've only a few months left until the wedding—but sexual temptations and sins are much simpler, if no less insidious, than other things. Things like grief or hatred or—the feeling that you're better than someone else. You doubtless wonder why all of us never liked your mother. Well, for the simple reason that she wasn't our type. And then your father died and she was still alive, and that didn't seem very just, now did it? And then, when faced with a great challenge, she folded up like an accordion. To people who've fought and won great battles in life, that seemed rather cowardly. So when you mix all of these things together, what do you have? A recipe for utter loathing and contempt. And one hard, if not impossible, to overcome."

The old man was silent, and in that silence a torrent of feelings flowed into Harry's brain: blind rage, which fought pity and sudden understanding until it was winded and the two more admirable qualities, for an instant, gained the ascendancy. Then his grandfather spoke again. "Of course, there's always Purgatory after we die for you and I and the rest of us to purge away our sins. But it seems a shame that we don't have the strength, or don't want to find the strength, to make matters right in our own lifetimes, doesn't it? Sometimes I wonder why God puts up with us at all. Perhaps He's the greatest sentimentalist."

"I don't know, grandfather," Harry said, regarding the old man with affection and without fear or anxiety for the first time in memory. "I don't know."

CHAPTER NINETEEN

The next morning, Sandra awoke to find that Mrs. McCreedy had had a bad night. "How many attacks did you have?" Sandra asked, her face pale, her eyes wide and staring.

"Three," Mrs. McCreedy whispered.

"When?"

"Twelve, one-thirty, and four. The nitro tablets made them go right away."

Sandra looked around frantically, as if some object in the room would tell her what to do. "Oh, my God," she finally gasped, and turned and hurried for the bedroom door. "You've got to take your medicine."

"Sandra, wait," the older woman begged.

"You've got to take your medicine!" Sandra cried.

"Please, darling, please wait. Come back here just a minute." With an anguished look on her face, Sandra complied. Her future mother-in-law took her feebly by the shoulders and, smiling sadly, looked into her eyes.

"Darling," she said, "you mustn't worry about me so much. If I die the next minute, I'll have lived more than most people live in a long lifetime. You need to be thinking about Harry, about your marriage and your life together. I appreciate your care—you've no idea how much it helps—but you need to think about your future."

Tears spilled down Sandra's cheeks from between her shut eyes. "I don't want to lose you," she moaned.

"I know. But you won't lose me. I'll always be watching out for you. Harry, too."

Sandra opened her eyes and wiped away some of her tears. "Really?" she asked, with a childlike eagerness.

"Of course. I'll be your guardian angel. I'll always pray for you and look after you. I don't know how much you're allowed to do things like that, once you cross over, but whatever I'm allowed to do, I'll do. And I'll pray for you every second."

Sandra burst out weeping anew and buried her face in Mrs.

McCreedy's shoulder. Mrs. McCreedy held her and rocked her and kissed her hair.

"Sandra," she asked after the younger woman had cried herself out, "what do I give back to you?"

Sandra wiped her face on the sleeve of her nightgown. "What do you mean?"

"You work so hard to care for me—what do you get out of it? I just wondered."

"Well, you're so dear—and you've had such a hard life— and you've suffered from depression, like me, but yours was so much more severe than mine. We've gone through the same fire together. That's such a powerful bond."

"And what else?"

Sandra sighed. "Well...this sounds so horribly selfish...but you need me. It's so nice to be needed."

"Darling, Harry needs you much more than I ever will."

"I know, but he can take care of himself. But you...really need me. I don't want you to be so dependent on me, I'd give my life if it would give you one day of health and freedom, but...it's so nice to be needed!" She curled up against Mrs. McCreedy, as if in shame.

"I know, darling," Mrs. McCreedy said. "I know. It is so wonderful to be needed, especially if you feel that no one needs you." She kissed the top of Sandra's head. "But Harry will always need you, Sandra. You'll always have someone to care for. Will you promise me that you'll always look after Harry?"

"*Always,*" Sandra said fiercely. "Always, Mrs. McCreedy, always."

Harry's mother smiled. "Good girl. And don't worry, it's not time for me to go yet. I didn't hear the end of Beethoven's Ninth."

"What?"

"I don't know why, but I've always known that when I die, I'll hear the last minute or so of Beethoven's Ninth Symphony. You're an intelligent and cultured girl—I'm sure you know the Ninth Symphony?"

"Yes, very well. It's one of my favorites."

93

"Well, you know how it ends—the music really cranks up and becomes very wild and frenzied, and then it comes to a really rousing end with those last three notes?"

Sandra hummed the ending of the piece to herself, and Mrs. McCreedy joined in on the last three notes. "Why, yes, I remember," she said.

"Well, this is going to sound crazy—but then we're both crazy, right?"

Sandra laughed.

"Those last three notes—sometimes orchestras play them really fast, and sometimes they take a little pause between them. I've never liked it when they play them fast—there should be a little restraint at the end. When they play them fast, it sounds so chaotic—like my mind felt when it was spinning out of control. But I love that piece so much, it sounds like the music of Heaven, and I love the sentiments it expresses—you know, 'Ode to Joy,' the brotherhood of Man, and all that. So when I die, I just know that I'm going to hear that piece. But I'm scared, because I don't know if there'll be pauses between those last three notes. If there aren't any pauses, that means I'll die in chaos and pain, and I won't get to Heaven, or everything I believed in will turn out to have been a lie—I know it. But if there's a pause, if it comes to a majestic and dignified end, then everything will be well. Of all the things in the world, that worries me the most. I don't know how those last three notes are going to be played."

CHAPTER TWENTY

A month passed. On St. Patrick's Day, Harry wore a green jacket in honor of the day. When he went into Sally's office to pick up some forms, she told him, "Nice jacket."

"Well, thank you," Harry said, surprised at the compliment. After two months of her sweetness-and-light act, Sally had reverted to her old self, and now barely spoke to him.

"It's real nice," she went on. "It looks nice on you."

"Well, thanks."

"So what you going to do with Sandra tonight?"

Harry, puzzled by Sally's sudden interest in him, paused a moment before answering. "We're going to the celebration at O'Flaherty's Irish Pub."

"That sounds like fun."

"I'm sure it will be."

There was a pause. Then she asked, "How do you think things are going around here?"

He weighed his reply carefully before giving it. "Why—very well, I imagine."

"It's going good for you, I know, so I guess you can't complain none." As she said this, she turned her face away and downward, as if in despair.

Harry decided to cut to the heart of the matter. "Sally, what's wrong?" he asked.

"Nothing, nothing," she mumbled.

"Something must be wrong. Please, Sally, tell me."

She sighed and looked at him. "Well, I thought that we were going to be partners. But all our plans have been fucked up, and I don't know who's to blame."

"How have they gone wrong?" Harry asked, though he knew the answer.

"Things are improving," she said, "and they didn't start improving until you came here. That makes it look like I was fucking things up. And that's going to look real bad for me." Her voice was husky, her eyes on the verge of filling with tears.

Harry was silent.

"What this means is," Sally continued, "that things are gonna be really bad for me at performance review time."

Harry could only shrug.

"I always wanted to be the best," she said. "I never knew how, but I always wanted to be the best. I took this job when I was eighteen, right out of high school, and I didn't know what the fuck I wanted to do with my life. I just had to do what I needed to survive. That's what most black folks got to do. I don't know about the rich Republican black folks you know, but us poor niggers got to struggle to make ends meet. And don't say that you're poor 'cause your family disowned you 'cause your mama went crazy. That don't matter. You still got that rich person's outlook, just like I got the poor nigger outlook. You can't get beyond it. It's like being born with no arms and legs, or with a face that looks like a pig. You're stuck with that outlook. But anyway, I went to work here, and tried to do the right thing, and I found that I was a good salesperson. So eventually I was promoted to where you are now—it took me a long time to get there, but you stepped right into it, that's what being a white guy with a college education gets you—and suddenly I found out that I had me some power.

"Whoooee! That was like having a vibrator buzzing against you nonstop twenty-four hours a day. I guess it went to my head a little. But hey, I deserved it, didn't I? I'd been living in shit for over twenty years, I wanted to get rid of the smell. But anyway, people were scared of me—me, this dumb nigger bitch—they wanted to do something besides fuck me now. And I did real well. I got promoted to manager in just two years—and don't tell me that it was because of affirmative action, Mr. Republican. When that happened, most of the people working here were white men and women. And white men and women may not like black women, but when one of us starts acting up, watch out! They run like rabbits being chased by hound dogs. If enough black women started acting up, they'd rule the world. White people would be cowering in their shithouses in fear. And that's the secret of my success.

"Now, we got a black man and a black woman working here, so they ain't scared of me at all. And we also got a young snotnosed white guy who don't give a shit about nothing, and two other white people—Richard and Bernice—and they were the only ones who were definitely scared shitless of me. And as a result, things were going pretty bad around here. I could just manage to keep some people around here scared enough to keep things running pretty well. That was as far as being intimidating could take me. So I figured that, when it came time for me to get another promotion, I'd tell management, 'Look, I did the best I could with what little I had. Now don't you think I deserve a promotion?' But then you came along, white boy, and changed all that. You did things that I couldn't do. I was doing my damnedest to disguise my limitations. Then you, you shit, you came along and exposed them to the light of day."

Her eyes filled with tears, her voice choked in her throat. "Now what am I gonna do? What am I gonna do?"

Suddenly Sally went over to him and put her hands on his shoulders. "Look, you've been doing what I told you, haven't you? You ain't been going around telling them to do better, have you?"

"No," Harry replied truthfully.

"Well, then, can't you go around and—tell them to fuck things up? Can't you do that?" She laid her hand reverently on Harry's right breast. "I'll make it worth your while," she said. "I'll pay you back. I'll pay you back good."

A tingling spread throughout Harry's body. He managed to let out a short, stifled gasp.

"So what you say, honey?" she asked as she slowly moved her hand down the length of his body. "What you say?"

He closed his eyes and marshaled his fear, forcing it to work toward action instead of paralysis. Then, with a short animal cry of determination, he pushed Sally aside and ran out of the office.

Harry leaned against the wall of the corridor and gasped for breath. When he had the strength, he would go outside. He needed some clean air; he needed a bath; he needed to lower his

97

already low opinion of the world and humanity. He crept to the water fountain and splashed his face with water. It felt so good and clean and pure, not like his own situation at all. It wasn't holy water, but it would do.

CHAPTER TWENTY-ONE

Harry told only Sandra about his encounter with Sally; she was furious and implored him to file charges against his boss. He vetoed the idea—that would ruin his master plan —but made a full written report on the event for the company president. This would surely be the final nail in Sally's coffin.

His twenty-third birthday on the twentieth of April afforded Harry much satisfaction. He had never liked the idea of being young, and had always looked forward to growing old; somehow, being twenty-three sounded much older than being twenty-two. Of course, people said that you could be young at forty or fifty or even sixty; but Harry knew better.

The scam at work played itself out as before. Sally actually seemed embarrassed by what she had done; at any rate, she regarded Harry with shamefaced silence for weeks afterward. The others dealt with her in their various ways and, in spite of her wishes, continued to improve personally and professionally. As April gave way to May and May inched toward June, the atmosphere at Port Arthur grew more pleasant, almost happy; everyone was united in the goal of overthrowing Sally. Everyone could barely wait for the coming of fall, when they would have the pleasure of kicking Sally after she had fallen into the dust.

CHAPTER TWENTY-TWO

Mrs. Trefontana was handling most of the wedding prepa-
rations. "You two don't know beans about organizing something
like a wedding. I'm organizing this, and that's *final*," she had
said, and Harry and Sandra were happy to let her do so. However, Sandra declared that Harry's mother, and not her own,
would help her pick out her wedding dress. Mrs. Trefontana was
a bit startled, but for some reason unknown to herself did not
protest. Harry's mother tried to beg off—"I've got terrible taste,"
she insisted—but Sandra, who was beginning to manage a good
imitation of her mother's imperious manner, would not hear of
it. "If you don't help me pick out my wedding dress," she announced, "then I'm getting married naked." So Mrs. McCreedy
relented.

The wedding Mass was set for one-thirty in the afternoon
on Saturday, the twenty-fourth of June. The reception would
follow at three o'clock in the church's reception hall. A disk jockey
would be there to play golden oldies, soft rock love songs, and
Italian opera arias. Then everyone would attend the Saturday
evening vigil Mass, and then Harry and Sandra would drive to a
supposedly haunted inn near Gettysburg, Pennsylvania, for their
weeklong honeymoon.

Plenty of Sandra's aunts and uncles and cousins were coming to the wedding; surprisingly, a number of Harry's relatives
were as well. Why were they coming, he wondered? Because his
grandfather had told them that Harry wasn't such a loser, after
all? Out of simple courtesy? Or did they feel genuinely sorry for
the way they had treated him? At any rate, they would all be
coming together to celebrate one of *his* great accomplishments.
It didn't seem possible.

Harry thought surprisingly little about the big day; he was
so wrapped up in the logistics of the thing that he had little time
to feel its spirit. Besides, getting married was a titanic undertaking that held within it all of the contradictions and vicissitudes
of life; like the nature of God, the human brain could not en-

compass it. All one could do was just *do* it, and then there would be a lifetime in which to reflect upon its meaning.

His mother, however, could think about little else. "It'll all be finished," she said dreamily. "I won't have to worry about you kids anymore."

"You worry about me, mother?" Harry asked.

"Oh, every minute," she replied. "All that time I was locked away, when I wasn't so crazy that I didn't know who I was, I thought about you all the time, and I knew how you must have been suffering much more than I was suffering. But I wasn't so much worried about your not having someone to look after you— of course, I was worried about that, too—but I was more worried about your not being able to look after me. You're a caregiver, Harry; that's your destiny. But everything turned out well in the end; you rescued me and you've been able to make the end of my life the most beautiful part of it. I've never been so happy as I've been these last few months. And you brought Sandra into my life, and she's been—she's a miracle. I've felt a bond with her that I've never felt with anyone else, except for you and your dad. She's so wonderful. But, sweetheart, it's her I'm worried about more than you."

"Why, mother?"

"Because she needs someone to look after her. She's someone whom God made for a caregiver like you to care for—that's her destiny. Oh, she's a very strong girl, and with your help she'll get much stronger. But she'll always need someone—you—to care for her. Just like it turned out that I needed you. She's taken such good care of me, but mine is a special situation—she can't keep that up forever, and once I'm gone, she'll be just devastated, devastated. She'll need you badly." She took her son's hands. "And Harry, I want you to promise me that you'll always look after her."

"I promise, mother."

"Good boy. I knew you would. You'll look after her for the rest of her life, because you're a good person. That's all I need to know, sweetheart, to die in peace."

Harry, weighed down by grief, bowed his head and slowly

lowered it into his mother's lap. She passed one claw over his head, while with the other she stroked his back. "Don't worry, baby. Everything will be fine as long as you have someone to care for. You saved me. You did more for me than anyone else ever has. Remember that."

Harry shuddered. Would this crippled but living flesh soon be cold and lifeless? Would he ever see her again? Would she even live to see him get married?

"As long as you can be a caregiver, you'll have a wonderful life," his mother went on. "And you'll be caring for Sandra—she deserves all your love and care. You'll have a beautiful life without me. And don't forget, if it's allowed, I'll be waiting for both of you when it's your time to join me. Then we'll never be apart again."

Her words wrenched Harry, and he started sobbing.

CHAPTER TWENTY-THREE

On Thursday, 22 June, Harry's coworkers held a luncheon in honor of his upcoming marriage at Harvey's. Everyone was there except for Sally, who pleaded a lame excuse. Harry was touched because he realized that, after almost a year of ceaseless anxiety, the daily grind of work, and many skullduggeries, he had inspired feelings of affection and respect in a group of human beings. He could be, at least in a small way, a leader of men, just like his revered ancestors, just like his father; he really could perform that most vital and difficult of worldly tasks, "getting along with other people."

Throughout the meal (Harry ordered a T-bone steak with baked potato, green peas, and rice), everyone offered him advice on how to succeed, in every way, at his marriage. "Just stay away from her when she has her period," Denise said, "and go down on her when you can't get it up. Then you'll do fine."

"Read the Bible every day," Frank advised. "You Catholics don't know the Bible very well, and don't sufficiently respect it as the cornerstone of salvation. If you get the Bible into your lives, then your union will be blessed."

"Just love one another and try not to get too mad at each other," Bernice told him. "Try to be forgiving of each other's faults."

"Has that worked for you, Bernice?" Harry asked.

"Well, I don't know how well my marriage has worked out, but it's been twenty-six years and we haven't killed each other yet. That's something."

Albert had nothing to say. "I think that anyone who gets married is crazy," he quipped with his patented air of indifference. "But apparently you share what psychologists call a collective madness, so maybe you'll get along all right."

"Oh, Albert, shut up!" Bernice said. "Be serious for once!"

"I am being serious," he replied. "I'm treating an insane world in an insane manner. If that isn't being serious, I don't know what is."

Bernice let out a groan and gave up. But Harry felt compelled for some reason to press the matter. "Do you have a girlfriend, Albert?" he asked.

"Yes. But we're certainly not going to get married."

"Well, maybe you just haven't found the right person yet. You're young; you still have time."

"Not much, if I went by your example—which I'm not."

"Well, I found the right person."

"Yes," Albert said mockingly. "She's...*wonderful.*"

Harry blushed with embarrassment and anger. "I don't sound that bad, do I?"

"No. You're worse. And it's enough to make you sick to your stomach."

"Oh, Albert, shut up!" Denise interjected. "Harry ain't that bad. He's just in love, is all."

"He's insane, is what he is."

"You never told me about your girlfriend," Harry said. "What's she like?"

"She's...wonderful."

Harry did something that he had never done in his entire life: he balled up his napkin and threw it at another human being.

"Oooh, temper, temper," Albert said. "All that sex you've been getting has given you a real wild-man complex. The next thing you know, you'll quit your job and become a commando."

The thought that anyone would consider him tough and macho, even facetiously, made Harry feel puffed up. "I just might at that," he replied.

"No, you won't. You're too afraid of life."

"What do you mean?"

"You seem like you're very afraid of life, Harry. You shouldn't be."

Harry tried to think of a means of responding to this undeniable truth. "Well, I certainly used to be," he said at last. "But I'm growing less afraid every day. I'm learning how to conquer my fears. You can't just make them go away in an instant, you know."

"You can if you've never been afraid," Albert rejoined.

"So you've never been afraid, eh?"

"Never. It's stupid, a waste of time."

Harry smiled sadly. "Well, I envy you your courage." He wanted to add, "If you really have any courage," but restrained himself.

"Thank you," Albert replied officiously.

"That's bullshit, Albert," Richard cut in. "You don't have any guts at all. You didn't want to take on Sally, and all the rest of us did."

"No, Richard, I just don't care enough about Sally to take her on. I'm not scared of her at all. What's the worst thing she can do to me? Call me names? Fire me? I don't care about those things. That's the difference between me and all of you. That's why I'm going to still be alive and enjoying life when the rest of you have heart attacks and die because you care what other people think too much."

"It's not a question of being sensitive," Richard countered. "It's a question of having pride. And self-respect. Nothing may mean anything in the end, but some things are worth taking a stand for. If you don't, then what's the point of living?"

"That's telling him, Richard," Harry chimed in.

Albert looked from one man to the other with a self-satisfied smirk. "You guys really think this bullshit's going to get you somewhere, don't you? Well, maybe we'll have to give you a little wake-up call one of these days."

At these words, Harry's nerves sang with terror. He looked questioningly at Richard, who returned his stare in like fashion. Was this Albert's way of saying that he was going to tell Sally about their little scheme? It couldn't be. Albert was all talk and no action; this was just another of his juvenile tricks. But still, he seemed to believe so passionately in his philosophy of indifference—perhaps enough to take active steps to prove it...

Lunch was soon over, and it was time for the toasts. Bernice made hers first. "Harry, you certainly gave all of us some hope when we had given up," she said. "Here's hoping that you'll have much hope for the future, and for your life with Sandra."

Everyone said, "Here, here," and drank.

Richard spoke next. "Harry, I went the same route as you, and it turned out to be a disaster. But I'm not so bitter or disillusioned that I don't know that things can turn out differently. Here's hoping that you have better luck than I did."

Then came Denise. "Harry, I can see how much knowing Sandra has changed you. I hope she always makes you happy, and vice versa. And I hope she always keeps you drained dry and never loses her ability to suck a golf ball through twenty feet of garden hose."

They all toasted this, except for Bernice, who cried, "Denise! Keep it down! People at the other tables can hear you."

"I don't care none," Denise replied.

Lastly came Frank. (Everyone knew better than to ask Albert to make a toast.) "May God bless you and keep you both, Harry. And may you always remember that sometimes the Lord wants you to get out your box cutter and fight back, just like my mama did."

Everyone was silent.

"What's wrong?" Frank asked.

"That's a sick suggestion," Bernice said. "We're not going to toast something like that."

"Well, shit, we're doing it to Sally now—figuratively, at least."

"Well, yeah," Richard agreed.

Harry stepped in. "Well, we'll toast what Frank said—figuratively."

Everyone did so.

CHAPTER TWENTY-FOUR

When Harry returned from the luncheon in his honor, he found a note on his desk: Sally wanted to see him. He felt a sinking feeling in his gut. Was she going to try to harass him again, or revert to her former role of tyrant? The large meal that he had just eaten churned in his stomach; he hoped that it wouldn't come up.

Why am I still so afraid? he wondered. I'm twenty-three years old now. I'm going to get married the day after tomorrow. I've proved that I can handle the world, that I can be in charge and not screw things up. I'm not a weakling, I'm a strong person, a doer. Then why am I still as frightened as I always was? Why is it impossible for me to change?

Harry tried to steel himself, to force iron into his soul. But it was no use; he felt his inner resources coming undone like a knot when the proper string is pulled.

He knocked on the door of Sally's office and heard her call out, "Come in." He did so, and sat down, and scrutinized her face closely. She was smiling; her manner was totally friendly. Harry's fear evaporated, to be replaced by a worse emotion, uncertainty. What on earth was she up to?

"Hey, Harry," she said in a cheerful voice. "How was the party?"

"Uh—it was fine," he replied. "It was very nice."

"That's good. Sorry I couldn't make it."

"That's quite all right."

"So, Harry, are you looking forward to the big day?"

"Well, yes, but at the moment I'm so busy getting ready for it that I don't have time to feel much about it, you know what I mean?"

"Yeah, it's always that way with big things. So, we'll miss you next week."

What was she doing? All of this sweetness must be a trap; she was leading up to something sinister. Harry said, "Oh, I'm sure that you'll all get along fine without me."

"Maybe, maybe not. But before you leave to go on your honeymoon, I wanted to tell you something."

Harry's heart stopped beating and expanded in his chest. *Here it comes*, he thought.

"I wanted to tell you that I'm real sorry for all the things I've done—treating you bad and all that. That was wrong. I'd like to apologize."

Everything inside Harry went limp. He stammered an incoherent reply.

"I really do want to apologize," Sally continued. "I really do. I'm just so…well, I don't mean to make excuses, but life is really hard for someone like me. It makes you all pissed off and suspicious of everyone—you start to think that the whole world's against you. You feel determined to get ahead and it don't matter who you got to step on to get there. That's how people in my situation who make anything of themselves feel, anyway. But it was wrong. And I've got you to thank for turning me around, Harry. You showed me that there's a better way of dealing with people. Shit, you turned this place around in a few months, and how did you do it? By having a good attitude and being nice to people. Just a little bit of good feeling, that's all it took. I see now that making things better is the only way to help myself, and other people, too. And I just wanted to thank you for that."

This can't happen, Harry thought. *People don't have sudden changes of heart. Not in real life.* He continued to listen in stunned silence.

She rose and extended her hand. "So, thank you, Harry, for helping to turn me around."

For a moment he sat in idiotic silence; then he got to his feet quickly and took her hand. "Sally," he managed to say, "I can't tell you how happy this has made me."

"Well, I'm the one who should be happy," she replied. "And you have a nice wedding and a good honeymoon."

"I will, thanks." He turned and left her office.

Out in the hallway, Harry tried to make sense of what he had just heard. If Sally's words were sincere, then he had witnessed a miracle. And he had helped bring it about. If Sally was lying, then she was plotting her most devious trick yet. But which could it be?

I mustn't be cynical, Harry thought. He wanted to believe that Sally had been telling the truth with all his heart. He wanted to believe that goodness—a rare commodity in this place, and in the world at large—had finally triumphed. Sally's behavior had not seemed like an act, but still something didn't seem right. He went to his tiny office, closed the door, and tried to think.

It was no use. He'd better pray. So he did, and felt better, but still unenlightened. He couldn't accept Sally's seeming conversion at face value. She would have to prove herself, over a long period of time, before he could wholly believe her. His mind made up, he walked out to the main show room.

He was just about to pass through the door leading to the show room when something caught his eye. He saw Sally and Albert at the end of the corridor, standing together and talking. Then something truly astonishing happened: Sally put her arms around Albert and embraced him.

In an instant, Harry understood everything. But they mustn't see him, and know that he knew. He hurried through the show room door.

So Albert had told Sally about their plan to bring her down. And she had put on this act of contrition to get them to change their minds.

An act, it had all been a well-played but cynical act. Harry felt a sickness in his gut, a sickness that he knew would linger for a very long time. He was disappointed, but hardly surprised. He must tell the others what Sally was up to.

But this store had been the scene of such discord—wouldn't it be nice to have a time of peace, even a false peace? Sally's phony transformation had surely come too late to save her; her sins, which had been dutifully recorded, were too many and too egregious. He hated the idea of deceiving people—although, come to think of it, hadn't he been deceiving Sally all these months?—but perhaps it would be best for everyone if he kept this knowledge to himself.

But no, Sally did not deserve to get away with this latest

and most monstrous of her lies. She did not have the right to think, even for a moment, that she had gotten away with it. What to do? That question hung in the air like a weight suspended by a thread that was quickly unraveling.

CHAPTER TWENTY-FIVE

After work, Harry went to Mrs. Trefontana's house in Arlington, where he and his mother and Sandra were "camping out" during the final days of preparation. Harry, of course, had no time to think of Sally's machinations and Albert's duplicity once he arrived home; the place was a circus, with Mrs. Trefontana the ringmaster. It was ten o'clock before things quieted down. Then Harry went to the guest bedroom to check on his mother and to ask her—for what? Advice? Her blessing? To see if she was still alive? He couldn't say. He merely wanted to be in her presence, and to hear her speak.

He found Sandra sitting up in bed with his mother and holding her hands. "Harry, go away," Sandra said. "I'm talking with my mommy."

Harry chuckled. "Well, she's my mother, too."

"Not anymore. My other mommy can adopt you. Go away."

Harry laughed and turned to leave, but his mother said, "No, wait a minute, baby. I need to talk with both of you. Is that okay, Sharon?"

Sharon adopted a look of mock disappointment. "Well, okay. But just for a minute...mommy."

Mrs. McCreedy laughed as loud as she could, which wasn't very, and replied, "All right...daughter."

Harry sat down on the bed, and his mother put an arm around him. "Harry—Sandra—I have a very selfish request to make," she said.

"You can have anything you want," Sandra said. "Name it."

She sighed. "Well, you know how weak I am now...I'm as happy as can be, but I just can't act very happy because...you know I don't have any energy, and these medicines I'm taking just make me feel like a zombie. And I want to...act happy for one day. I want to be my old self again, especially on Saturday of all days. I want to—well, there's only one way that I can act that way."

Suddenly Harry understood. "You mean…?"

"Yes, baby, I…as horrible as this sounds, I know the only way I'll be able to really cut loose and act happy will be if I…well, get drunk. When I had my breakdown, the only way that I could stay sane and keep on taking care of you was if I got drunk. You remember, baby, how that was. And…it was so wonderful, being able to be at least partly my old self again and have some strength to face the world. But then I went into the hospital, and they wouldn't let me drink anymore. And…well, this is the result." She paused, an anguished look on her face. "And I wanted to ask you kids' permission…I know it's stupid and I shouldn't drink when I'm taking all these medications…but if it's all right with you, could I please get good and drunk on Saturday so that I can be my old self one more time before I die, and really act out all the joy I feel inside?"

Memories of the past assaulted Harry, of how light-hearted and vivacious and alive his mother had once been. He did not want to remember, his present equanimity demanded that he not remember, but he did anyway.

"Of course, mother," he said in a choked voice. "You go right ahead." He needed to run away and hide, to be besieged by these memories in some private place. So he hugged his mother and buried his face against her neck as the pain stabbed him again and again.

Sandra's face was red from the tears that were flowing down it. "Oh, Mrs. McCreedy!" she moaned, and sought refuge against Harry's mother's other shoulder.

Mrs. McCreedy took in a deep breath, as though savoring the aroma of her coming liberation, and began to rock her two grieving children (for so they seemed to her) slowly back and forth. Softly, the words to her favorite lullaby rose to her lips:

Cobwebs and dust will be there tomorrow,
But babies grow up, we've learned to our sorrow.
So cobwebs be quiet! Dust go to sleep!
I'm rocking my baby, 'cause babies don't keep.

CHAPTER TWENTY-SIX

The wedding rehearsal went smoothly, and afterward Harry, Sandra, and their mothers went to a party that Harry's family was throwing for him in the banquet hall of the Willard Hotel—a sort of "Welcome Harry Back to the Family Party," as the guest of honor called it ruefully. Amazingly, his family all treated him not just with civility, but with affection, as if he had never been an outcast. Even Aunt Susan, his most vicious tormentor, treated him like a star in the family firmament. "You're all right, Harry," she said, patting his cheek with one of the hands with which she had formerly slapped and pummeled him. "Maybe you do take after your father, after all."

Harry looked her in the eyes and, incredibly, was no longer afraid of her. Her abuse no longer mattered; perhaps it, along with everything else, had never mattered in the first place. "I must have inherited it," he replied. For a long time he had rejected the family's mantra that everything about a person was inherited, but he was coming to accept it more and more, although he could never be a genetic absolutist. Then, incredibly, Aunt Susan put her arms around him and gave him a kiss.

Throughout the proceedings, Sandra—who looked absolutely beautiful in a white evening dress with thin shoulder straps—smiled and radiated charm. Hers was not a polished charm; her feelings, long imprisoned by shyness and fear, had only recently been liberated and were still new to her, not yet malleable to the conscious shaping and artful employment that make for polished charm. Hers was the overflowing enthusiasm of a young woman in love for the first time, and it spilled over onto everyone present, even the members of Harry's family whom she despised for their treatment of Harry and his mother. When Harry's grandfather came up and took her hand, she smiled brightly and said, "I'm so glad you could come."

The old man looked over at Harry's mother, who was receiving the reluctant greetings of her late husband's family with a bright smile, then looked back at Sandra. He paused for a moment, and actually glanced down at the floor, then said, "I understand that you want me to say something to Harry's mother, that you're angry with me because of how I feel about her."

"Can't you go over and say something to her?" Sandra asked. "She's right over there. Honestly, is your dislike of her so important that you can't be nice to her today, on such a happy day?"

The old gentleman sighed. "All right, my dear," he said. "I'll do it for you."

Sandra's face was transported with joy. She pulled Harry's grandfather to her and hugged him tightly, then planted a hard, loud kiss on each of his cheeks. He was startled but pleased, and gave a little smile, then walked slowly over to his daughter-in-law.

Harry's mother saw him approach and smiled. Even before he reached her, she held out her crippled hand and said, "Oh, granddad"—that had always been her pet name for him—"I'm so glad to see you."

He took her hand and made a little bow. "Hello, Elizabeth," he said with forced cordiality. "How are you?"

"Oh," she said breathlessly, "I've never been so happy." She patted the empty chair beside her. "Please sit down, granddad. I have so much to tell you."

The old man paused for an instant, then forced himself to sit down beside her. She threaded her two weak arms through one of his strong ones and then, softly but eagerly, began to speak and did not stop for the rest of the evening.

"I can't believe it," Harry said later. "Grandfather's actually talking to mother. Well, actually, she's doing most of the talking." He was silent for a moment. "But that's the way she is. She's a very forgiving person."

Sandra put an arm around his shoulders and kissed him. "Yes, isn't she great? You know, Harry, maybe that's why we were brought together. So that your whole family could be reunited."

"That could well be," he said.

"Will you look at mother, buttering up all of your rich relatives like she's the queen of Park Avenue. She is *such* a social climber."

"Oh, she's cute," Harry said. "Don't mind her."

"I was just talking to your cousin Frank. He says he asked you to join the new business that he's starting."

"Yes, he did. And it's very tempting. In fact, I told him that I probably would take him up on it, but that I had to wait until after September, when the performance reviews come up." He smiled. "Sandra, who's being a social climber now? You want to have a rich entrepreneur husband, huh?"

"Harry, no," she said seriously. "I'd love you if you were a blind man selling pencils on a street corner. But you'd fit in much better at a place like that, with your talents and education. For so much of your life, you had to settle for nothing. From now on, I want you to settle for nothing but the best."

"I won't, darling. But I promised myself and the others that I'd see this thing through. If I give up on it now, I'll never be able to live with myself."

"Hey!" Sandra cried. "A remark like that is supposed to elicit a comment like, 'I've already got the best—I've got you.' Well! Some gallant husband *you* are!"

He laughed and hugged her and smiled as he remembered his conversation with Frank. Frank, an energetic young redhead only five years Harry's senior, had already made a fortune in business and was clearly the star of his generation of the family. "The old man was telling me about all the crap you're taking from the people you work with," Frank had said. "Come work with me."

"That would be nice," he had replied.

"So why don't you come on board?"

"I have to wait until after September, when the performance reviews come up, and...I suppose grandfather told you about the little coup I've planned?"

"Yeah, and it took balls to think that up, but you're wasting your time on a bunch of losers. Are you sure you made a promise to people who are worth keeping your promises to?"

"Yes," Harry replied without hesitation. "Yes, I did."

"Well, okay, but, really, Harry...don't you want to be part of something big?"

"Yes, I do, and I will be. But I have an obligation to keep first. But, Frank, your making this offer to me—and I'm sure I'll take it—means more to me than you can possibly know. Even more than grandfather's telling me that, if I proved myself, he might make a place for me in the family business."

"Screw the old man! His way of doing business is gone. In five years, he'll be asking us for money."

Yes, Harry wanted to have his hand on the levers that ran the world. And Frank had assured him that the job would still be open after September. He would accept the offer then, but for now, all that mattered was getting Sally fired and bringing peace to Port Arthur Shoes.

CHAPTER TWENTY-SEVEN

That same evening, Richard, Frank, Denise, and Bernice, all of whom had been invited to the wedding and had agreed to go, met at Bernice's home in a modest Maryland suburb.

"You know," Bernice said, "I'm so shocked by the way Sally's been acting over the last few days that I could almost believe she really has had a change of heart."

"That woman is bad to the bone," Frank countered. "She has a devil in her. The only way you can change that woman is to have an exorcism." Everyone else laughed, but Frank explained, "I'm serious. That woman's got a devil in her. I've never performed an exorcism myself, but my mama did, many times, and I witnessed enough of her exorcisms to know that demons do take possession of people. That's the cause of so much of the evil in the world, but people don't realize it. So many times when people say, 'He's got a devil in him,' they're speaking the truth. That woman, she's let all sorts of demons come into her. It would take a month or two to drive them all out."

The others tried hard, but unsuccessfully, to hide their amused skepticism. Frank saw the suppressed smiles on their faces and said, "Laugh if you want. But the devil's taken over Sally's soul, and he's waging war on all of us. I finally realized that. We've got to fight the devil the only way you can fight him."

Richard asked, "What are we going to do—kidnap her and hold her hostage until you drive all the demons out?"

"I think that's the only thing that will work."

"Oh, Frank, talk sense!" Bernice said. "She doesn't have a devil in her, she acts like a devil because she chooses to. And we're going to exorcise her by getting her fired. It's that simple."

Frank shrugged. "All right, be that way if you want. But the devil's going to take possession of all of you before this is over with, just wait and see."

"Look who's talking," Denise quipped.

"And what do you mean by that?" he demanded.

"Frank, you're always judging people and talking about how

your mama cut up some woman 'cause she said some of us really are niggers. Sounds like you've got more than a few devils in you, to me."

"Damnit, that's different!" he cried. "My mama was standing up against the forces of evil, just like she did when she drove out demons. God is a God of judgment as well as love, you know, no matter what them heathens who call themselves Christians say. And if you don't stand up as a weapon of God's judgment, then God will judge you."

"All right, Frank, we get your point," Richard said. "Now let's get back to business."

"I was talking about business," Frank sulked. "The Lord's business. But okay, you want to be that way, that's fine."

"So," Richard said, "are we all agreed that we're not taken in by this new bullshit act of Sally's and that, while on the surface we'll be nice to her, we're going to go ahead and nail her in September with all the documentation we have?"

Everyone agreed.

"I wish Harry was here," Denise said. "It seems wrong to have a conference like this without him being here. He started all this, and he's guided us through everything—it seems like we'll fuck things up without him."

"So you're letting a white man do all your thinking for you?" Frank asked. "You think you're just a dumb black bitch who needs a white man to tell her what to do?"

Fire flashed in Denise's eyes, and she sprang to her feet. "You shut your stupid-ass mouth!" she cried, pointing a finger at him.

"Hey, hey!" Bernice yelled, stepping between them. "We're not going to have any of this!"

"That woman's stupid," Frank cried. "She's so dumb she thinks she needs a white man to do her thinking for her."

"I ain't dumb!" Denise cried. "You the one that's dumb. You the one that thinks you know what God wants better than God does. You the one whose dick's so small you got to admire your mama slicing someone up with a box cutter to make your dick feel big."

"GODDAMNIT, I'LL KILL HER!" Frank cried, and lunged for Denise. Bernice tried to hold him back; the effort nearly bent her in half. Richard hurried up and wrapped his beefy arms around Frank's chest. This held him fast, but still Frank kicked and screamed like an animal caught in a snare. "You making fun of the Lord and my mama. You're gonna pay, you're gonna pay!"

"STOP THIS!" Richard yelled. "STOP THIS!"

"Yeah, you a big man," Denise taunted. "You're so stupid that you don't even know when to take good advice. You so stupid you don't even know when you're doing the devil's work, fool! You know, that lady your mama cut up—"

"DENISE!" Bernice cried in terror. "That's enough!"

Slowly, Richard managed to maneuver his kicking, cursing burden toward the front door; when he finally reached the door, Bernice opened it, and then Richard shoved Frank outside with a snarled command to "Get out of here!"

"And don't come back!" Bernice added as she slammed the door in Frank's face. Then she slumped against the wall and gasped for breath. *"Jesus,"* she said.

"I'm writing a report about him," Richard said. "That guy's sick. If they don't take care of him, he'll kill somebody."

"I'm writing one too," Bernice gasped.

"Me, too," Denise added.

"What's happening to us?" Bernice asked. "What's happening to us?"

"Sally's hate," Denise said. "Hate is the easiest virus in the world to catch, as my preacher used to say." She chuckled. "Of course, Frank would probably say that my preacher didn't know what he was talking about—"

"Fuck him," Richard muttered.

"Good advice, Richard," she said.

Bernice shuffled over to the couch, sat down, leaned her head back, and pressed her hands to her eyes in a futile effort to stem the pain throbbing behind them. "Maybe this is wrong," she said after a long pause. "Maybe Harry was right."

"What do you mean?" Denise asked.

"A couple of months ago, Harry said to me that he could be a successful dictator if he wanted to. I asked him what he meant and he said, 'A successful dictator has to give the public a scapegoat—someone to hate. Sometimes I feel like that's what I'm doing with you guys and Sally.' He was joking, but maybe he was right. Maybe we should just give this up and let Sally pull her shit on us. Fighting back just seems to poison us all. I thought we were all getting along so well, and now this happens. Everything that woman touches gets poisoned. If you do nothing, then she poisons you with her hate. If you fight back, then you start turning into her. Maybe we should all just quit—run away—start over somewhere else."

"If we do that, then she really will have won," Richard protested. "We've got to keep on doing what we're doing. If we let her get away with it, if we give in, then she really will have poisoned us."

"He's right," Denise said. "We can't let her win. There's a right way and a wrong way to deal with her, and Mr. Shit-for-Brains Frank don't realize that. That's all."

"I'm not so sure," Bernice replied. "Before we started fighting back we were miserable, but…nothing like this."

"And it's because she made us miserable that we're acting like this," Richard said. "You can't keep that inside forever. When Harry made us realize that we had to fight back, of course we started acting like this. It's the price of being abused. And that's why we've got to take a stand against Sally before she destroys us. I'm no theologian like Frank, but I can't believe that God would want us to be abused."

"That's right," Denise said.

Bernice sighed. "I guess you're right. But I just can't shake the idea that maybe Harry wasn't joking, that he was telling the truth. He gave us…Sally…to hate."

"We already hated Sally," Richard pointed out.

"Yes. But he wanted to help us, so he gave us…permission, in a way…to *really* hate her. But it's wrong. Maybe it's wrong. We shouldn't hate at all. We should just get out of that place and away from that evil woman as fast as we can."

"And how are we going to put food on the table and keep a roof over our heads?" Richard demanded.

Bernice had no answer.

CHAPTER TWENTY-EIGHT

Frank was locked out. The swift, purifying flood of his rage had been cut off in mid-stream, and its suddenly damned-up power sent him into a convulsive fit. He stomped his feet, gnashed his jaws, and struck out at the air. He turned to look back at the door that was closed and locked against him and felt the sudden urge to smash his fist through it, to break down the barrier between him and the people whom he had been trying to help, to reach, even though they would not listen to his message.

He stomped down the driveway to the street, where his car was parked beside the curb. The frustrated rage was now centered in his skull; his brain felt swollen with anger, as if it would soon explode. He stopped and gritted his teeth, trying to master his wrath. He couldn't do it; his brain throbbed, throbbed with madness, sending spurts of destructive energy down into his limbs. It had to find release through action, so he stomped off down the street on a walk that would take him God knew where, that would last for God knew how long.

The rage had been with him all his life. He had not been born with it, he was certain of that. His mother had taught it to him; she had shown him from his earliest days how to rage against the devil.

His mother had hated sin, injustice, and weakness. From his days in the cradle she had taught him to hate those things, as well. The world had to be set right, both outwardly and inwardly. This was not, she thought, a task for each individual to handle in his own way, through prayer and the diligent living of a proper life; that was a doctrine taught by the heathens who called themselves Christians, who wanted to observe the social niceties rather than preach the Gospel of God. And preaching that Gospel meant constantly shaking things up; it meant getting in people's faces, hurting their feelings, and striking back at the first sign of aggression. Jesus may have preached love and forgiveness, but He was still the incarnation of the old God of the Israelites, who consumed thousands of people with fire at the least provocation. Vengeance was the Lord's, it was true, but those who truly walked with God could become the messengers of His vengeance, as well as His love.

Frank had heeded his mother's message; he had been born a frightened, timid child, and the idea of becoming a strong messenger of the mighty God made him feel powerful and secure. Besides, his mother would beat him mercilessly at the slightest display of weakness on his part, so being strong kept his body safe, as well. And he had been a most successful soldier of the Lord. By the age of fifteen, he had become a minister in the small church that his mother and some of her associates had founded. But if he prospered as a minister, he failed in just about everything else. He was expelled from several schools for fighting—the ignorant heathens who ran the places couldn't understand that the children he fought had insulted him, or his race, or the Gospel that he preached. And the Lord did not forgive you if you allowed people who mocked His message to go unchallenged.

People sometimes told Frank that he was not serving God at all but his own raging, wounded ego. He was distorting the Gospel, they said, so that he could justify his own atrocious behavior. This accusation had given him pause the first few times he heard it, and he had pondered over it, but not for long. If God didn't want you to be strong, if He wanted you to be weak and despised of your fellow men, then how could He be a loving God? If He didn't want His teachings to be defended, then how could He say that those teachings were true and holy? Then the world would be a cold, frightening, and hateful place; then God might as well be the devil, and oblivion the only hope of reaching Heaven. But no, it couldn't be; his God was not a coward, and neither was he, who had been created in God's image.

Frank had planned to become a full-time preacher when he grew up, but his mother's death of cancer, conflicts and power struggles within his mother's church, and his own depleted funds had forced him into the business world. Still, he planned to realize his goal, once he had saved up enough money, of starting his own church. And the business world did give him plenty of opportunities to meet, and evangelize, large groups of people. This proselytizing had gotten him fired on more than one occasion, and so eventually, God forgive him, he had toned it down somewhat. And then along came Sally. She was the most formidable opponent he had ever dealt with, and since he couldn't afford to be fired again, he could not lash out physically or verbally at her. And so Sally knew that she could get away with persecuting him. Luckily, he could take his frustrations out on Albert, an equally aggravating but much less formidable thorn in his side. Then Harry had arrived, and had tried to make things better. That formerly rich white boy had some good ideas, Frank had to admit, but he was too timid; he didn't want to strike back with the mail-clad fist of God's vengeance. It was that heathen Catholic religion that he put so much faith in; it had reduced him to a meek, servile little vassal. That was how the Catholic religion, and most other perversions of God's word, operated: they needed their flocks to be servile and obedient, so they kept them in a state of constant fear and taught them to turn the other cheek, to return good for evil, and other corrupted versions of Jesus's misunderstood teachings.

Frank could not endure it. He would fight back against that evil bitch Sally in his own way. To hell with Harry and his "proper way" of doing things.

Still, he couldn't afford to be fired again. Performance reviews were just three months off. Perhaps he could put his conscience on hold for a while longer. But he was a man and a soldier of God, not a little worm waiting to be crushed underfoot. He had fought for his mother's—and God's—teachings for too long to compromise them further. Besides, he was going to make a horrendous spiritual compromise tomorrow—going into a temple of Catholic idolatry to attend Harry's wedding—and that was enough compromise for one lifetime.

Frank had walked over a dozen blocks by this time, and his anger, like his strength and his wind, was starting to subside. He stopped, leaned against a lamppost, and tried to regain his breath. He prayed to God for guidance. The answer came to him almost instantly: he would go along with Harry's plan for now, for the sake of peace. The plan would surely result in Sally getting fired; even in the crazy world of Port Arthur Shoes, simple justice had to prevail, didn't it? But if it didn't, then he would enforce God's own justice. And he would hold nothing back.

He felt the boxcutter in his pocket. It comforted him.

CHAPTER TWENTY-NINE

"Dear children of God," the officiating priest, Father O'Matteny, said in the middle of the wedding Mass, "brothers and sisters in Christ: we are here today to solemnize and commemorate a sacrifice—not only the Holy Sacrifice of the Mass, but also the sacrifice of two people who are relinquishing their individuality to become, as the Scriptures say, 'one flesh.' For marriage is a sacrifice, a dying to one's self in order to live for another, a replacement of two separate, alienated beings with a fuller, united being, a two-in-one.

"From this moment on, Harry and Sandra will be not just lone disciples of Christ, but also disciples of each other. They must serve and obey one another in commemoration of Our Lord, in Whose Image they were created, and Whom they were created to know, serve, and love. In so doing they will serve as a constant reminder to each other of how best to know, serve, and love their Creator, but they will also remind one another of the selfless love of that selfsame Creator, who abandoned His throne of glory in Heaven to take the form of sinful man and win back His dearly loved creatures to Himself. When Our Lord was a child, He was obedient to His parents, and in so doing He not only taught children to be obedient to their earthly parents; He also enabled those obedient children to teach their parents how to be obedient, in turn, to God, their Heavenly Father. So it is with Harry and Sally, and with all of God's children who enter into the Holy Sacrament of Matrimony.

"Some misguided souls have said that the Scriptures, and the Sacrament of Matrimony, support the subjugation of women because the bride promises to 'obey' her husband. Well, had they ever bothered to consult the entire passage from Ephesians in which this injunction is laid upon women, they would see that the Apostle Paul lays an equally stern injunction upon husbands to love their wives and to subsume their interests to those of their better halves. And if children are urged to obey their parents, so are parents urged to love their children, to treat them kindly, and not to provoke them. And if servants are enjoined to obey their masters, so are masters enjoined to honor their servants. Some have said that this passage supports the institution of slavery. But in truth, there is no stronger condemnation in all of human thought and writing of that barbaric practice, and no more moving affirmation of the freedom that all men can and must enjoy under God.

"In a moment, we will approach the altar and commingle our body and blood with the Body and Blood of Christ. When we do this, as Our Lord commanded us to do, we, in effect, become one with Him—one flesh with Our Lord. So, in like fashion, are Harry and Sally approaching the altar today to symbolize that divine practice on a human level—to become one flesh with each other."

Harry was so moved by Father O'Matteny's words that tears nearly came to his eyes, and he just managed to suppress them. He was more prone to tears than the average man, but still regarded shedding tears in public as unmanly. Sandra had no such compunctions, and her tears flowed freely and unashamedly down her cheeks.

The rest of the ceremony was a blur. There seemed no need to linger over its every detail; he and Sandra were being joined together, as they were meant to be, and that was all that mattered. In like fashion, when Harry knelt at the Communion rail and the priest placed the Host on his tongue, Harry did not, as before, feel terribly unworthy or force himself to think of the terrible solemnity of the occasion; God and he belonged together, just like he and Sandra, and that was that. Did Sandra feel the same? He looked over at her; her face was trembling with happiness, and tears were still running down it. Surely she was experiencing her moment of epiphany, as well.

The reception afterward was a whirl of laughter, dancing, and good wishes, as raucous as the ceremony had been reverent. Harry's mother had gotten thoroughly drunk that morning, and was her old self again—merry and witty and full of energy, bustling around the room, managing everything, talking with and kissing everybody, even those who hated her. At one point she dragged Harry's Aunt Susan over to the bride and groom and said, "Will you look at that? How could a crazy woman like me have such a wonderful son like that?"

"I have no idea, Elizabeth," Susan replied tartly.

"Oh, you're impossible," she said, and gave her a long, hard kiss on the cheek that made Susan wince. "But I love you anyway."

She spent most of her time talking with Grandfather McCreedy or with Mrs. Trefontana, who had agreed to look after her while their children were on their honeymoon. "I know that you don't have a lot of patience for people with my condition, that it makes you nervous," she told Sandra's mother. "And I know that Sandra gave you strict orders not to make any jokes about my problem. But if you want to make fun of me, that's okay. I'm tough—I can take it."

Mrs. Trefontana, for once, was at a loss for words—seemed overwhelmed with embarrassment, in fact.

Harry's mother laughed. "Oh, you are such a silly! Really, I'm looking forward to staying with you next week. I'm mean, our kids are married now, and it's such a beautiful union they have, so we really need to get better acquainted."

"That's true," Mrs. Trefontana agreed, then added with more than a touch of resentment, "Sandra really loves you."

"And you're jealous of that, right? Oh, honey, don't be. I mean, I'm going to die soon anyway, so then I'll be out of the way and you won't have anyone to be jealous of anymore!" She laughed uproariously. "But, seriously, Sandra loves you very much. And Harry does, too. He admires you very much, he's told me so. And I have a feeling that Harry and Sandra will come to depend upon you very much, after I'm gone." She took Mrs. Trefontana's hand. "Do you promise me that you'll look after them and take good care of my babies for me?"

Mrs. Trefontana laughed in turn. "I'm an Italian mother from Brooklyn. What do you think?"

"Oh, I'm so glad," Harry's mother said, and the two women embraced. Then she looked Sandra's mother straight in the eyes and continued, "But listen. I know you don't like the Irish. Do you know what my maiden name is? Sullivan."

Sandra's mother flinched and turned red with shame, and looked from side to side, as if searching for an escape route.

"And when I'm gone, I'll be watching over the kids, like I promised I would, and if you ever don't take care of my babies or are mean to them, then I'll come back from the dead and pound your sorry wop carcass into the pavement."

Mrs. Trefontana had recovered her composure, and greeted this threat with a smile. "I could always lick the Irish," she said, "but I promise anyway."

The two women burst out laughing, and passed in an instant from polite acquaintances to the best of friends.

The party and the dancing went on throughout the afternoon; then it was time for the Saturday evening vigil Mass, which all of the partygoers attended, even Frank, who frequently had to stifle laughter as he observed, for the second time in a day, the absurdities of this pagan ritual. His soul felt secure—nothing this ridiculous could ever corrupt it. Then at last it was time for the newlyweds to drive to the allegedly haunted Cashtown Inn near Gettysburg. Before they got into Harry's car, their mothers detained them for a long moment with hugs and kisses and blessings.

"Sandra," Harry's mother said in a sudden moment of solemnity, "I don't want you to be worried about me while you're away."

"Oh...I'll try not to," Sandra replied.

"I know you're worried that I'll have a heart attack and die while you're away. Don't be, dear. I know God won't let me die while you're away. And please don't feel guilty—I know you feel guilty. I know that, deep down, a part of you is thinking, 'That woman better not die while we're away and spoil our honeymoon!' It's human nature not to want anything to spoil such a happy event. And you love me so much that you feel guilty about being selfish. Well, you *deserve* to be selfish about this. And if I'm so thoughtless as to die and interrupt your honeymoon, then I deserve all the criticism you can heap upon me."

"Oh, Mrs. McCreedy!" Sandra wailed, and held her new

mother-in-law tightly. Harry, similarly affected, and humbled as well by such selflessness, turned away and got out his handkerchief.

"Harry, Sandra, stop blubbering!" cried Mrs. Trefontana, who seemed a little moved herself. "You're married now. You've got to be strong for each other. This is no time for hysterics. Besides, even if something does happen to Elizabeth, she won't really be gone—she'll just be with the Cuban."

Puzzled, the others looked at her.

"Haven't you heard that joke?" Mrs. Trefontana asked. "You know how Hispanics pronounce Our Lord's name Hay-seuss, not Jee-sus? Anyway, this man says to his friend, 'My wife's run off with another man!'

"'That's terrible!' his friend says. 'How did that happen?'

"The guy says, 'My wife had to go into the hospital for an operation, and then this Puerto Rican nurse comes out and says to me, 'I'm sorry, your wife's gone, but don't be sad—she's with Hay-seuss.'

"'Hay-seuss?' the friend asks. 'Who's Hay-seuss?'

"'I don't know, but whoever He is...that Cuban has my wife!'"

Giddiness replaced sorrow, and they all collapsed in laughter.

CHAPTER THIRTY

Harry and Sandra spent a great deal of their honeymoon at the Cashtown Inn simply holding each other and trying to get used to the miraculous fact that they were, finally, one. That they had found and been united with each other was—well, it was positively humbling.

They made love, of course, countless times, and it was much better than before. There was a delicious new intensity to the act that defied explanation; its initiation was simpler and more natural, its culmination more vigorous. Furthermore, each had adopted a possessive attitude toward the other that made their lovemaking seem not a delightful novelty, but the natural order of things—an entitlement, even. When Harry mounted Sandra or when Sandra rubbed up against him and began to kiss, fondle, bite, suck, and lick, it was as if they were saying, "I need you, and I deserve you—now comfort me, as you promised."

The newlyweds spent part of their honeymoon taking in the local attractions—the Gettysburg battlefield, the shrine of St. Elizabeth Ann Seton in nearby Parsonsburg, the town of Gettysburg itself. At Sandra's insistence, they checked in on Harry's mother every day; after recovering from her monumental hangover, she was doing fine. Every day Sandra would say, "Mrs. McCreedy, are you sure mom's not insulting you or giving you a hard time?" and "Mom, remember you promised that you wouldn't say a word against Harry's mother." Both women would laughingly assure her that they were getting along famously, as in fact they were.

They returned home on the evening of Monday, 3 July—they had stayed an extra day to see all of the reenactments of the Battle of Gettysburg—and on the following day, they took their mothers to the Fourth of July celebrations. Then Wednesday arrived, and they headed back to work.

Sandra's first action upon returning to her job was to ensure that the nameplate on her desk and all her other forms of identification were changed immediately to reflect her new name,

Sandra McCreedy. "I'm married now," she said. "I'm a new person, I'm a member of Harry's family, and I want the whole world to know it." Her female colleagues, amazed that Sandra had finally found a husband, let alone one so much younger, wanted to know every detail of her honeymoon. "Darling, please," she would invariably, and coyly, reply. "If I have to relive every lovely detail, we'll all get so excited that we won't be able to get any work done."

Harry's first task upon returning to work was to determine how much damage Sally had or had not done in his absence. Luckily, she had accomplished nothing; she was still trying to drown everyone in a deluge of sweetness, but they were not buying it. They treated her politely, but kept her at arm's length. Harry was tremendously relieved. It was, he thought, foolish to keep the news about Sally and Albert a secret any longer, and so he told his colleagues, one by one, what he had seen. They were not surprised, but agreed upon one thing: from this point on, Albert was to be treated as if he didn't exist.

Richard told Harry of Frank's recent explosion. This alarmed Harry greatly, even filled him with a sense of dread. He knew that Frank was an unstable, volatile character, but until now, he had never really thought that Frank's anger would find release in actual violence. Now he knew that this was not only possible, but perhaps inevitable.

What could he do? As a professional, he had to take action against violence, or potential violence, in the workplace. On the other hand he hated turning on Frank, since he had enlisted him in the campaign against Sally. How could he keep collecting Frank's reports while at the same time plotting Frank's own downfall?

Perhaps, Harry thought, he could postpone dealing with the Frank problem until he had resolved the Sally problem. But no, he had to protect his coworkers against the threat of violence. Also (he thought in a moment of self-preservation), if word leaked out that he had known of Frank's potential for violence and had done nothing about it, it would harm his career. So what to do?

Harry sent up a prayer to St. Michael as the cords of others' madness and guile, and his own dishonest attempt to redeem things, tightened around him.

CHAPTER THIRTY-ONE

"Just when I thought that I'd put everything in its proper place," Harry told Sandra, "someone opens a window and the wind blows everything askew."

Harry was lying on the couch, and Sandra was giving him a back rub. "I know, you poor darling," she murmured. "But you're strong. I know you can handle it."

"I'm glad you think that," he said. "But I don't know what to do. If I turn against Frank, then I'll feel like a traitor. If I don't turn against him, then I'll be acting irresponsibly. Fine choice, huh?"

She moved her hands to the center of his back and began to massage his spine. Harry groaned; it seemed as if she were cleaning the detritus from the center of his being. "Sweetheart..." Sandra began.

"You think I should take the job that my cousin Frank offered me now?" Harry asked.

"Well...I guess really, no. You have to keep your word, and you're an honorable man. It wouldn't be the honorable thing to do. I could never ask you to do something dishonorable."

"Well, I've made my decision. As soon as the performance reviews come through in September, I'm resigning. Then I'll go to work for Frank."

"Really?" Sandra asked with girlish excitement.

"Yes."

Sandra embraced him. "Oh, darling, I'm so happy for you! Finally you're going to be at a place that's worthy of you, and you're going to be respected, and you're going to earn what you deserve—oh, Harry, I'm so happy!" She pressed her kisses into his cheeks.

"Well, hold on," he said, chuckling. "We have to get through this thing first."

"Oh, that doesn't matter. In two months, you're going to be free of that dreadful place. It's wonderful!" She kissed him on the mouth. "I've worried about you being stuck there so much that I almost feel like I'm getting out of jail myself!"

He laughed and asked, "What about that back rub?"

"Oh, gosh, I forgot!"

She resumed her massage. Then Harry noticed his mother sitting in a chair on the balcony, writing with the careful intensity of a medieval scribe. "What's mother doing?" he asked.

Sandra flinched, and her mood changed from gay to grim. "She's writing us letters," she said.

"Letters?"

"One letter for each of us. To be opened…after she's…" She could not go on, and put her head in her hands.

Harry tried to pull Sandra to him, but suddenly she snapped out of her grief and pinned his arms down. "No!" she cried. "I was supposed to make you feel better."

"But honey—"

"She's your mother, and you're about to lose her, and I should be comforting you. It's obscene, your comforting me when it's much more your loss than mine."

"She means as much to you as she does to me."

"That's true. But you've done so much for me and I do almost nothing for you. That's got to change. I've got to start doing more for you than you do for me—not that that's possible, but still, I've got to try."

Harry's patience snapped. "Sandra, stop it! This is a partnership. We both help and comfort each other. Neither of us has a monopoly on giving or receiving it. We're equals. Can't you get that through your thick head?"

Sandra was startled for an instant; then she smiled that toothy smile that had won Harry over at their first meeting. "You're right," she said. "And yes, even my thick skull can take that in. You know, I keep forgetting how young you are. You seem so much older than me, somehow." She leaned down and kissed him, then said, "One super-perfect back rub coming right up."

CHAPTER THIRTY-TWO

The following day, Harry summoned Frank into his office and closed the door behind them.

"What's up?" Frank asked.

"A big problem, Frank," Harry replied. "Sit down."

Frank looked anxious. "What is it?"

"Just sit down, and I'll tell you."

Frank did so, and Harry sat down in turn, let out a deep sigh, forced himself to look directly into Frank's eyes and to adopt a sad, benevolent expression, and began, "Frank—I'm really concerned about your temper."

"What about it?" Frank asked, honestly surprised.

"I'm scared that it could...well...get out of hand."

"What, are you scared that I'll cut someone with a box cutter like my mama did?"

"Well, yeah, that's exactly it, as a matter of fact."

Frank laughed. "Harry, you don't have anything to worry about. No one here's done anything to deserve that—not yet, anyway."

"That's exactly what I mean, Frank! The fact that you don't immediately come out and say, 'Oh, no, I'd never do that to a soul in a million years' raises the possibility that it *could* happen."

Frank eyed him suspiciously. "How come you're worried about this all of a sudden?"

"Because of what happened at the meeting you guys had on the night before my wedding."

His wary look immediately became hard and dark with anger. "Did those guys tell on me?"

"Well, yes."

"Damnit!" he cried, slapping his fist hard against his thigh. "Damn them squealers!"

"Frank, calm down!" Harry cried in turn, struggling unsuccessfully to keep his own rising anger out of his voice. "I'm trying to help you!"

"Yeah? How are you trying to do that?"

"Because I haven't reported you yet, that's why!"

Frank fell silent. His eyes widened in amazement. "You haven't?" he asked after a moment.

"No. The others who were at the meeting have already written you up. I haven't yet, because I felt guilty about...well, informing on you when I've already enlisted you to inform on Sally. But I couldn't just let it go, because I've got an obligation to report on the possibility that a coworker might engage in violence in the workplace. That's part of my job. If I let it go, then not only am I not doing my job, I could get in very big trouble. So do you see my dilemma?" Frank didn't answer, so Harry went on, "So here's what I've decided to do. I'm going to have to do a report about you, but I wanted to have this talk with you first so you wouldn't think that I went behind your back and did it. And, if you agree to what I'm going to say, then I can put a whole different spin on this. And it will make Sally look bad, not you, because I can say that this is the kind of work environment that she created. I can say that you acted that way because of the stress that Sally created around here. Do you follow me?"

"I think so," Frank replied, astonished at Harry's generosity.

"Good. Well, what I propose is this: You promise that you won't lose your temper *at all* until the problem of Sally is resolved. You formally apologize to Denise for losing your temper at her. You continue to work with us on getting rid of Sally, who I think you agree is our main problem. Then I'll go ahead and write up a report on this, giving it the spin that I described to you. I'll put it in the Sally file, and that will be another very big piece of ammunition to use against her. Do you understand it all? Is that okay?"

The very winning smile that Frank could, on occasion, display spread across his face. "Harry, that's the slickest thing I've ever heard!" he exclaimed. "You should be a lawyer."

"Nah, business is my life's work. So we're agreed?"

"Well, I'll try to hold my temper, and I'll apologize to Denise. She's a good girl. She just lets her mouth run away from her brain sometimes."

Look who's talking, Harry thought. But he merely said, "Good man. So the work place is now safer, my obligation is fulfilled, and my rear end is covered."

"You know, Harry, you're a good person at heart. You're all right."

"Why, thank you, Frank," Harry replied, touched.

"You went to bat for me. You were honest with me and tried to help me when you could have just gone behind my back. I can't remember the last time when someone did something like that for me. You're all right, man." He rose and extended a hand to Harry, who rose in turn and shook it.

"So we're friends now?" Harry asked. "We know where each other is coming from, and we're working toward the same goal?"

"We sure are. But just one thing, Harry—if all of this goes wrong, then I'm going to be more pissed at you than I've ever been at anyone in my whole life."

Harry gave a delighted laugh. "Frank, there's no way this is going to fail."

CHAPTER THIRTY-THREE

Sally's behavior at work was still impeccable—she seemingly treated everyone with a newfound respect and courtesy—but there were signs that her façade was crumbling. She looked at people warily, as if they might assault her at any minute. When she spoke, there was a tremor in her voice that threatened to push it into a higher register or break it altogether. Everyone knew that she was frightened of the approaching performance reviews, when all of the accumulated evidence against her would be brought forth, and she knew that they knew. Life at Port Arthur became a weird dance of the transfer of power. Every day Sally would ask people how they were doing, while at the same time voicing the unspoken plea, "Please don't do this to me; please let me off the hook." They would reply that they were doing fine, while also silently letting her know, "There will be no mercy; the day of reckoning is at hand."

Then, on the morning of Monday, the seventh of August, Harry received a phone call from Sally. "Harry, I've got the flu," she said in a voice thick with suffering, or with feigned suffering, Harry couldn't be sure which. "The doctor's told me that I have to stay in bed all week. You and Bernice will have to hold down the fort until I get better."

"I'm sorry to hear about that," Harry replied with glib concern. "I hope you get better soon."

"Yeah, I do, too," Sally mumbled, and hung up.

When Harry relayed this news to his coworkers, they all greeted it with derisive snorts. "Flu, my ass!" Richard exclaimed. "Scared shitless is more like it."

Harry chuckled. "As always, Richard, you hit the nail right on the head."

Denise said, "She's probably sick, all right, but it wasn't caused by flu germs. It was caused by Harry McCreedy."

The idea of having such an effect on another's physical body—violating and destroying it, in effect—shook Harry and filled him with guilt. "Don't be silly," he said.

"It was you. Just like the AIDS virus, except she got the HMC virus."

"Denise, come on!" Harry said, a little louder than he intended.

She laid a hand on his arm. The touch was surprisingly intimate, and Harry was astonished. Then he looked into Denise's eyes to see what lurked there. Nothing did; only the upturned corners of her mouth spoke of something significant, and hidden. Then she removed her hand and walked away.

Harry stared down at his arm, which still tingled from the touch of Denise's hand. Did Denise really like him in that way? He didn't know what to think, wasn't even sure that he wanted to. He looked up again and watched her depart, along with the answer to this mystery, another in the endless parade of riddles that life threw your way to keep you off balance, or flat on your face.

Bernice, however, was worried about Sally's purported illness. "She's up to something," she told Harry. "I don't know what, but she's up to something."

"What could she possibly do?" Harry asked.

"I don't know. Go to the president and offer him a blow job if he'll ignore everything we've said against her, maybe."

Harry laughed. "Bernice, I didn't know that you were a conspiracy theorist."

"I'm not being paranoid. I wouldn't put anything past that bitch. She's been practically coming on to all of us these past few weeks, and it didn't work, so why shouldn't she move up the ladder and come on to the president?"

"Well, that's possible, but I don't know if she has that much guile left in reserve. She seems pretty beaten down to me." A sudden wave of remorse swept over Harry as he spoke these words. Perhaps, he thought, they could show a little mercy toward Sally.

But that was impossible. The course was set, and Sally had chosen her own fate. There was nothing he or any of them could do.

"You underestimate her," Bernice replied. "That woman is evil to the bone. She could get away with murder if they caught her doing it on videotape."

Harry's sense of pity was replaced by a chill of fear. Perhaps Sally *was* planning something. His old childhood feeling of being a bug about to be squashed by a large boot returned, or rather an echo of it did; he was now convinced enough of his own strength to keep that feeling somewhat at bay, but not to banish it completely.

Just then Albert, their resident Brutus, came hurrying up. "Harry, your wife's on the phone," he said in his nasal drone. "She needs to speak to you right away."

Immediately Harry sensed what the call was about. It couldn't be, not now, he didn't yet have the strength to withstand this particular blow. "Did she say what it was about?" he asked in a strangled voice.

"No," Albert replied; his voice had never grated so horribly on Harry's nerves. "But she sounded really upset."

It was time, Harry knew. The long period of waiting, of enjoying a blessed reprieve, was over. There was nothing he could do; an immense weight bore down on his soul. He hurried to the phone, his heart pounding faster with every step he took.

He reached the phone and almost shouted into the receiver, "Hello?"

"Harry?" Sandra's voice was low, frightened, choked with tears. "I'm at the hospital. Your mother's had a heart attack. They don't think—oh, Harry, we can't lose her so soon!" She burst into heartrending sobs.

"I'll be right there, honey," he promised. He was about to hang up the phone when he realized, to his horror, that Sandra hadn't mentioned which hospital his mother was at. He asked, "Honey, they did take her to the hospital she normally goes to— Holy Innocents Hospital?"

"Yes!" Sandra wailed through her sobs.

"I'll be right there! Don't worry!" He hung up the phone and headed for the front door.

Bernice hurried up and walked alongside him. "Harry, what's wrong?" she asked with a look of great, and genuine, concern.

"My mother's had a heart attack," he said. "They've taken her to the hospital. I have to go there."

"Oh, my God!" Bernice gasped. "I'll pray for her."

"Please do. I'll see you later." Harry ran through the front door and out onto the sidewalk, where he frantically hailed a taxi. Finally one stopped, and Harry told the driver, "Holy Innocents Hospital, and hurry." He began to mumble a silent, incoherent prayer, a prayer of unvoiced groans and whimpers rather than words. The overcast sky had cast a sick, gray pall over everything, as if corruption reigned and every living thing had begun its inevitable fall into decay.

CHAPTER THIRTY-FOUR

The taxi soon arrived at Holy Innocents Hospital, and Harry hurried to the information desk. Efficiently and without emotion, the woman at the desk told him which room his mother was in: room 457. Harry half-ran, half-stumbled to the elevator, whose doors took forever to open, and then rode it up to the fourth floor. The large vehicle quivered as it rose; with grief at its passenger's impending loss, Harry fancied. When the doors opened, Harry followed the signs down one particular corridor to room 457.

Sandra's mother was waiting in the hallway. "Oh, Harry, thank God you're here," she said. Her eyes were red from crying; she really had grown to care for his mother, Harry noted, and was thankful for that small mercy.

"What did they say?" he asked breathlessly.

She let out a deep sigh and gently took hold of his arms. "Sweetheart, your mother is going to die. They said they can't do anything."

Harry didn't know what to think; perhaps he would know if someone held him. Slowly, almost cautiously, he put his arms around Mrs. Trefontana, who in turn crushed him to her.

"Oh, my son, my new son, I'm so sorry," she said. "Your heart must be breaking. Oh, Harry, baby." Mrs. Trefontana began to cry.

Instinctively, Harry began to stroke his mother-in-law's back and murmur, "There, there."

She pulled back and said, "Harry, your mother's in there, you'd better go see her. And Sandra's there..." A look of utter terror came into her eyes. "Harry, this is going to *kill* Sharon. It's going to shatter her like a piece of crystal. Please, please don't let her go crazy again...you promised..." She put her hands to her face and sobbed.

Harry kissed her forehead and went into the room.

His mother, dressed in a hospital smock and looking pale and shriveled, lay on the bed; wires ran from under her smock to a heart monitor in a corner of the room. Its indicator showed that his mother's heart was still beating, but for how long? Sandra sat in a chair beside the bed, stroking his mother's right arm and hair and talking to her softly.

"Sweetheart, I promise that I'll look after Harry," she was saying. "You were right, I do need him…I'll need him more than ever after you're gone…but I swear that I'll look after him. Every last ounce of love that I had for you I'll transfer right over to him. And I already love him more than life itself, so think of how loved he'll be!"

Harry wanted to comfort Sandra, but he couldn't interrupt her last conversation with his mother—and it *was* a conversation. Somehow he knew that his mother heard Sandra's words—or, perhaps, already knew them. He pulled up a chair on the opposite side of the bed, sat down, and took his mother's crippled hand. It was not cold; she was still alive. He did not weep; his grief was already embedded in the marrow of his bones, so there was no need for him to cry. He looked at his mother's shriveled claw resting in his own hands and realized that, somehow, this symbolized their relationship perfectly. She had been locked away from him for so many empty years; then he had found her again, still alive but not for long. Their long and sad but beautiful history had come down to this. The world was a pair of entwined hands, and it was enough.

"Can you hear me, darling?" Sandra asked his mother. "Do you know that Harry and I are here with you? Can you feel us holding you? You're not alone. You're dying surrounded by people who love you more than life itself. You're not crazy anymore. You're not locked up. You're free—you're loved—isn't that the most incredible thing? You have all the love you wanted, all the love you deserve. You're not abandoned anymore. Do you understand that, darling? Do you feel it?"

Mrs. Trefontana, armed with her rosary, quietly entered the room, knelt down at the foot of the bed, crossed herself, and began to recite the rosary. Harry listened and, in a dull, silent way, occasionally joined in. Sandra continued to talk to his mother.

"I used to be so terrified of life. But I'll never be frightened again. You'll be my guardian angel, won't you, darling? Of course you will. You promised me you would, and you'd never lie to me. Oh, darling, please forgive me for being so selfish—I know you're going to be in Heaven where you'll be reunited with your husband, where you'll be so well and healthy and happy that you'd never want to come back here—but, oh, darling, I want you to stay here with us for a little while longer so badly. If you only knew what joy you brought us. Oh, darling, I can't help being selfish, please ask God to let you stay here with us a little longer!"

Soon Father O'Matteny arrived, recited the old Latin prayers, and anointed his mother. After he left, Sandra resumed her conversation.

"Oh, darling, you're all ready to go now, aren't you? You're going to go straight to Heaven, and you're never going to be in pain again. I'm sorry I was so selfish, wanting you to stay here. I'll—I'll try to get along without you—please help me, won't you? I promise I'll be strong for Harry, like you would want me to be. Like you were. They said you were weak, but you didn't let them kill you, darling. You were so strong. Your love, your forgiveness—they didn't kill them. They were stronger than ever before! Do you know what a great blessing seeing that was for me? It was like Harry's love and understanding. It made me see what Heaven was like. It brought a bit of Heaven down to earth, to me, when I was so lonely. You saved me, darling. You and Harry saved me. God bless you, darling—I'll try so hard to be as good and strong and loving and forgiving as you are."

Harry's mother heard Sandra's words. They reached her and were a balm to her soul. She had been preparing for this moment for the past year and more, and she was pretty sure that she was ready; but still, as her physical body began to die with frightening rapidity and as the chaotic, racing final chords of Beethoven's Ninth enveloped her in their whirlwind, she needed all the comfort she could get.

She had always maintained that it was the spirit, not the physical body, that mattered; but now, as one part of her after another died, winnowing her down to that vital spark, she realized how much life was bound up with physicality, what a great part of one's existence it was. The part of her that she knew would live on was—why, it was no bigger than a dot of light, like the fairies in those old illustrations. Once the rest of her was gone it would fly away like a sprite that had taken possession of her mortal body for a time but was now going back to its own kingdom, a place so far beyond the realm of mortal comprehension that the mortal senses could only wonder idly at its existence. But where would that vital spark go?

Jesus, she prayed, *where are You? Lord, will You accept me?* Most of the vast and unimportant parts of her were gone; death was closing in on her like a tightening fist, as the music crashed louder and louder in her ears. The chaos that had always terrified her and that had consumed too much of her life was waiting outside her diminishing frame of existence, crying, *I want you.* She cried out again, *Jesus, where are You? Will You take me?*

The last bits of her physical life died, and she was alone in the darkness. Suddenly the music was reigned in somewhat as it throbbed toward its climax. Mrs. McCreedy's vital spark quailed and waited in horror. How the last three notes were played, she knew, would determine where she was going. *Please let them be distinct,* she prayed, *with a tiny pause in between them, the way they're supposed to be played…*

The chaos was over. The first of the final three notes sounded distinct and firm, like an enormous period dropped down at the end of a too-long and chaotic sentence; then there was a pause, and another period dropped down; then another pause, and then the final, echoing period.

Her vital spark sent up a prayer of thanks and escaped from its dead shell and this sphere of being, where everything was born in violence and died. It did not falter in its journey; somehow it knew exactly where to go.

CHAPTER THIRTY-FIVE

Harry knew when his mother was dead because the room suddenly seemed emptier, as if one of the four people in it had walked out. He could not bear to look at the heart monitor for another moment—his eyes had been carefully avoiding it—but when at last he did so, he saw the line repeatedly making a straight journey from left to right. Funny, her hand was still warm and pliable. He looked down at the hand, then raised it to his lips and kissed it.

Mrs. Trefontana rose to her feet and crossed herself, then hurried over to Sandra, who was no longer talking with her mother-in-law but was still stroking her hair. She laid a hand gently on Sandra's shoulder. Sandra looked up in horror. "No!" she gasped. "She can't be gone yet!"

Mrs. Trefontana sobbed and said quietly, "Sandra, honey, she's gone."

Sandra's face twisted and compressed itself into a mask of anguish. She was on the verge of an unbearable outpouring of grief yet, horribly, was frozen in the instant before grief breaks forth. She looked at Harry, whose sad face confirmed the unthinkable. "No!" she said in a choking wail.

Her mother knelt beside her and put her arms around her. "Oh, sweetheart, it's a terrible blow..."

Sandra's body heaved with a stifled sob. Her shaking hands rose inch by inch toward her face, while her head began an equally slow descent toward her knees. Another stifled sob shook her body, then another, and another. Mrs. Trefontana cast an agonized and imploring look at Harry. In an instant, he sprang over and took Sandra in his arms. She was trembling so violently that it was hard to tell which would prove more terrible—the trembling or the explosion of grief that it foretold. Seconds passed, then a moment, yet, horribly, Sandra's grief remained locked within her. Finally, in despair, Harry let her go. What could he do?

"Oh, God, Harry, please help her," Mrs. Trefontana

moaned.

"Sandra, honey—" Harry began.

Sandra let out a sudden, sharp gasp. Both Harry and her mother jumped. "She kissed me!" Sandra cried, her face suddenly transfigured with wonder. "She just kissed me! I felt her!" She wrapped her arms around herself. "She's holding me! I can feel her holding me! And her hands—they're strong and soft. They're not crippled anymore!"

Mrs. Trefontana grabbed Harry's arm and cried, "Oh, Harry, she's going crazy!"

Sandra looked at Harry and her mother. "She touched me! She's all right! And she's still caring for me!"

Somehow, Harry knew this was not the madness of grief. He looked Sandra in the eyes and tried to speak. "Really?" was all he could say.

Sandra reached out and clutched his hands. "She's touching me!" she cried. "She's touching me, and I can feel her happiness. It's flowing from her into me. And I think I'll die, from feeling all this happiness! It's—not possible, to feel such happiness! And she'll feel that way forever and ever! Oh, Harry—she's *free!*" She pulled Harry to her in a crushing hug. "Oh, Harry, she's free! She's free! Isn't it wonderful?"

Free. What a strange word for anyone to utter in this life. An end to all obligations, to all pain, to all of the maddening promises of a better life tomorrow, always tomorrow, with which life kept you crawling along on your bloodied knees. He believed that his mother had gone to a better, freer world, but for some of the happiness of that world to seep through the veil into this one? It didn't seem possible. He collapsed atop his mother's body and began to sob violently, like an animal in pain.

Mrs. Trefontana slowly, timidly approached. "Sandra?" she asked in a quavering voice. "Are you—are you sure you're not crazy, baby?"

Sandra looked at her mother and smiled beatifically. "I'm not crazy, mother," she said.

Her mother put her hands to her mouth and stifled the faint cry of surprise and joy that issued from it. For a long time she did not move, but only watched as Sandra comforted the sobbing Harry; finally she realized that she had to do something, and got down on her knees and awkwardly put her arms around both of them. But she was too filled with joy at Sandra's deliverance to offer much consolation. Sandra had not been shattered by grief. It didn't make sense. She had often heard of miracles, but had never truly seen one before. She sat there dazed, and might have been dead like Elizabeth for all the thinking she could do.

The next three days passed in a numb, hushed blur. There was the visitation at the funeral home; Harry was comforted and found the strength to endure when he saw his mother lying in her casket with a look of supernal peace and beauty on her face. Then came the flight to Boston for the funeral Mass, which Father O'Matteny conducted. As it was an old-fashioned funeral Mass, the priest wore black robes instead of white, and no comforting prayers of hope but rather the gloomy *Dies Irae* was chanted, with its almost cringing pleas to be freed from the Judgment and Hellfire. Oddly, Harry and Sandra and Mrs. Trefontana found this more comforting than they would have the new, more upbeat Catholic funeral service. It was well to think of how terrible death was, how far from grace man had fallen, and how terrible was the wrath from which God had spared His children.

A surprising number of Harry's family came to the funeral, including Grandfather McCreedy, who solemnly informed Harry and Sandra that he had killed his feud with Elizabeth over a month ago, and it was time to bury it along with her. Harry felt a sense of relief at these words, while Sandra hugged the old man and covered his face with kisses.

They buried his mother next to his father in the family plot in Boston, amid several centuries of McCreedys and their kin by marriage. But something else went into the ground with his mother, something whose loss threatened to be even more terrible. While she lived, Harry had possessed a remarkably strong and automatic ability to endure grief, no matter how profound, because he had always believed that things would get better someday. And they had, beyond his wildest dreams. But now that his mother was dead, it was no longer possible for him to be resilient. Whatever future horrors life held in store for him, it would now be impossible to ignore their knife thrusts to his heart. He had no defenses left.

CHAPTER THIRTY-SIX

Harry returned to work on the Friday after his mother's death. Everyone was generous but sincere with expressions of sympathy, and Harry welcomed them gratefully. But what of the future? What new horrors did the world have in store for him now that the source of his strength had been taken away?

When Harry asked his coworkers how they had gotten along without Sally, they replied that of course it had been the most productive and least stressful week that any of them could remember. And how was Sally doing? Still sick in bed, the last they had heard, and she didn't expect to return until next Monday, or even Tuesday.

When Monday arrived with no sign of Sally, Harry called her at home. "Hello?" she asked in the voice of a perfectly healthy person.

"Sally? It's Harry."

"Oh, hey, Harry. How are you doing?"

"Fine, thanks."

"I'm sorry about your mother. I know she meant a lot to you."

"I appreciate that."

"So what are you calling about?"

"I was just wondering how you were doing."

"Oh, I'm all right now. I was just taking one more day off so that I could run some errands that piled up while I was sick."

Sick with fear, you mean, Harry thought. He said, "I'm glad that you're better."

"Thanks. Is anything going wrong at work?"

"No," Harry said, struggling to conceal his delight at being able to tell her this news. "Everything's fine."

"Well, that's good. Harry—"

"Yes?"

"Are you worried about the performance reviews?"

Well, of all the transparent— he thought, but replied, "No, not at all."

Sally's voice was low and bewildered: "I am."

Harry couldn't think of what to say.

"I worked really hard to get to where I am," Sally went on. "I never thought that I'd get this far. I just had to kind of make things up as I went along, know what I mean? And I'm scared that it's all going to amount to nothing."

For a moment Harry felt a sudden, overwhelming pity for Sally, and was almost ready to confess everything and burn the documents. "I'm sorry, Sally," he managed to say.

"Yeah," she said bitterly. "I am, too. Fat lot of good that does either of us."

"Sally, I—" he began, then stopped. *This is a game*, he told himself, *she's trying to manipulate you into giving up, don't get too close to her or she'll have you in her clutches.*

"What?" Sally asked.

"Nothing," he said.

She sighed. "What am I gonna *do?*"

"Sally, I…I don't know. That's up to you."

"Maybe I should pray about it some more. I've been praying about it for a long time."

"That's an excellent idea, Sally." Maybe there was hope for her yet.

"The trouble is, I'm scared that God's mad at me. I had to do a lot of bad things to get to where I am, and I'm scared that God's mad at me."

Harry tried to think of something to say. "Well…you don't have to be afraid of Him, Sally."

"I really do. I've had to do some really awful things in my life, but it was that or get plowed under. Do you see what I mean?"

Harry paused. *Don't answer*, he told himself, *this is a trap.* But he couldn't help saying, "Yes."

"So you do understand," Sally said in a queerly altered, almost mystical tone of voice. "That's good. Well, I'll see you tomorrow. Thanks for calling, Harry."

"Uh—my pleasure. Goodbye."

He hung up and tried to think this over. This was another

of Sally's tricks, it had to be. But her voice had sounded so sincere—her anguish might have been his own—her history was his history. They had merely taken different paths. Sally's path had led to ruin, his to success.

Harry unlocked his bottom drawer, where he had stowed all of the written evidence against Sally. It was a formidable pile, over a foot thick, the accumulation of days, weeks, months of cruelty, pettiness, and emotional violence. The record cried out for vengeance. Yet Sally's cruelty had—perhaps—been born in circumstances that he could well understand. In condemning her, he would be betraying a part of himself.

Harry sighed. He could not back out of this now, not after he had given the others his word and worked with them for so long. The hammer would have to fall upon Sally. There was no other choice.

But perhaps there was something that he could do to ease the blow? Something that would let Sally know he understood?

Stop being ridiculous, he scolded himself. *You don't even know that she was telling the truth. Are you going to be a patsy for that woman?*

He said a prayer and thought hard for a moment. Then a compromise occurred to him. It was perfect, why hadn't he thought of it at once? He turned to his computer keyboard and typed out his final report, which related the conversation he had just had with Sally. He ended by noting that, while she had sounded sincere, Sally had deceived him so often in the past that he couldn't be certain she was telling the truth. "Nevertheless," he wrote, "I certainly hope that she was telling the truth, and while her personal problems do not excuse her behavior at work, I hope that she will learn from this experience and do better in the future."

He proofread and signed the report, then added it to the pile of evidence. Then he phoned a shipping clerk at Port Arthur's administrative offices on Constitution Avenue. "I have a very big package that I need to send to the president," he said. "Could you come over on a special delivery run and pick it up?"

"Sure," the man replied. "I'll leave right now."

"Thank you so much."

"No problem."

Harry rose from his desk and went to tell the others that the fight was over, that they needn't write any more reports about Sally. They need only endure for a few more weeks, until the company president gave them the gift of her head.

CHAPTER THIRTY-SEVEN

Sally returned to Port Arthur the following day, Tuesday, 15 August, looking like she had just lost every member of her family. She had little energy and shuffled around the store like an invalid, addressing people in a dull, lethargic voice. The only parts of her with any life left in them were her eyes, which darted constantly from side to side and only rarely fixed themselves upon people. This made sense to Harry; a person who had gone to such extremes to do evil had much to fear. Others at the store were not so impressed.

"It's an act," Richard said. "That girl has more acts than a stand-up comic."

"She's sad, all right," Bernice opined, "but she's exaggerating it to try and get us to feel sorry for her."

"She's always full of shit," said Denise.

Albert, as always, had a different point of view. "I think she's really upset, and I think that you guys are so happy about it that you're having two orgasms a minute."

Harry rejoiced inwardly that Albert's barbs no longer troubled him in the slightest. "Albert, if you knew how wrong you are, you'd cry."

"Really?" Albert asked with feigned surprise.

"Yes." Acting on a sudden impulse, Harry added, "And you can tell Sally that if you like."

For a moment, Albert actually looked startled; then he shook his head vigorously, as if clearing the cobwebs from his brain, and once again donned his mask of youthful arrogance. "I don't know what you're talking about," he said.

"Don't you?" Harry asked.

"Have you been taking your lithium lately, Harry? You're getting paranoid."

Harry sighed. "Albert, you can't act this way forever. You've got to grow up someday."

"I know," Albert said seriously. "But being young and thinking that you know everything is fun. I figure that I've got a year or two left before I become an old man—like you."

"Albert," Harry said coldly, "I saw you talking with Denise. I know that you're telling on us behind our backs."

"All right, I did do that. So what? Harry, I'm only twenty-one years old and I know that this job is crap. You all act like it's the greatest job in the world. If all of you had any guts, you'd tell Sally off to her face and quit and go out and find yourselves real jobs. Working here is the best that any of you can do? And at least two of you have college degrees? Richard has a *doctorate*, for God's sake. Sounds pretty pathetic to me."

Harry allowed his anger to boil over. "Who gave you the right to judge what's pathetic and what's not? Who gave you the right to look down on people who've lived longer than you have and have gone through things you can't even imagine? Who gave you the right?"

Albert gave a wry grin. "I plead guilty to being inexperienced. But what gives you the right to act like you're some big Democrat who's got something in common with these people? Now that your crazy mother is dead and you've shown that you do have some balls, your rich family will take you back with open arms. Do you seriously think that you'll ever invite any of us into your home? Do you think that you'll ever invite us to any of your big parties? Wake up, Harry. In a little while, you'll be living in some other world a million miles away from the rest of us. Would you ever dream of having anything else to do with us?"

"Yes!" Harry cried, and added forcefully but without menace, "And don't insult my mother."

"Sorry," Albert replied flippantly. "I apologize. But you actually say you'd have us in your home?"

"Yes! If any of you want to come, you're welcome to."

"Well, hooray for you." He paused. "I don't know why I'm telling you this, but—Sally isn't all broken up about your campaign against her."

"Oh?" Harry asked.

"Yes. Everything she's ever done around here—being a hard-ass, being all sweet and contrite, acting all devastated—is just an act. Actually, she's grateful to you for getting her out of here. She told me so herself."

"Uh…what?" Harry stammered. He had never expected something like this, never.

"She hates it here. Did she tell you some bullshit about wanting to get promoted? That's not true. She's never going to get promoted again. The company president hates her. He met her once right after she was promoted to general manager and hated her attitude so much that he said she'd never get promoted again. And Sally doesn't even want to get promoted. She hates this place. She treats us the way she does because she's bored, and because she thinks we're low-class trash. Her family has a lot of money, you know—you two have something in common."

"They do?" Harry asked, astonished.

"Yes. Her family's worth a fortune. She doesn't want any-one here to know about it, because she thinks that if she keeps up her I'm-a-poor-oppressed-black-woman act, then everyone will be afraid to criticize her, but her family's probably worth more than yours is. A couple of weeks ago she invited me to a party at her father's house. It was a fucking mansion! It must have had twenty rooms, and it was in the middle of a forest that her father owned, too. If your campaign gets her fired, she won't starve—she won't even be out of a job. Her dad promised her that she could have a job with his company—some overseas dis-tribution firm—when she turned thirty, but he wanted her to work out in the real world until then to get some experience. I can't tell you how pissed off she was about that. Why do you think she was out all last week? She went home to her parents and gave them some song-and-dance about how the white people here are oppressing her and spreading lies to get her fired, and her father was so outraged that he offered her a job with him, even though she's not thirty yet. She's just staying here until the performance reviews next month so that when the president tells her that she's fired, she can say, 'I quit!'"

"And you know all this for sure?" Harry asked.

"She told me about it last night. We go for drinks after work sometimes. She was all happy that she's getting out of this place, and that she won't have to wait a few more years to go and work for her dad. So you see, Harry? You put all this effort into defeating her and it turns out that you were doing her a favor. It was all for nothing."

Harry sagged on his feet. His face was a mask of shock. Such deviousness, such cruelty in the service of such pettiness, didn't seem possible. A new vista opened up before him.

"Don't you see?" Albert pressed. "It was all for nothing."

"No," Harry replied suddenly, with quiet conviction. "It wasn't for nothing. We took a stand against something wrong, and we did it honorably, and we're going to get rid of the thing that's wrong. We did the right thing. That's all that matters."

Albert raised his hands in an "I give up" gesture. "Anyway, I just thought you'd like to know that. See you later." He began to walk away.

"Albert, wait," Harry said. "Why did you tell me all this, really?"

"I have no idea," the youth replied. "Certainly not because I have any respect for you. I don't, so don't look forward to taking long showers with me."

"Never, Albert. But thanks."

"No problem." Albert walked away.

For the first time since his mother's death, Harry felt a measure of security—not wholly secure, he would probably never feel that way again, but he felt a sense of being shielded somewhat from life's treacheries by the steel armor of knowing that he had done the right thing. He stood up straight. His survival was by no means assured, but perhaps he would be able to endure for a while longer.

CHAPTER THIRTY-EIGHT

That evening, Harry went with his wife and mother-in-law to church for the Feast of the Assumption. Then they went out to dinner to celebrate the beginning of the end of Harry's grand campaign against Sally. They were given a table with four chairs grouped around it, and the sight of that empty fourth chair filled Harry with sadness. "I wish that mother could have lived to see this," he said quietly.

"She is seeing it," Sandra assured him gently, laying a hand on his arm. "She's watching over us, just like she promised."

"I know," he said, "but it still makes me sad."

"I know. And there's no shame in that, darling. I cry my eyes out about her at least once a day. You know that she's at peace, but you miss her. There's nothing wrong with that."

Mrs. Trefontana reached across the table and took Harry's hand. "Those who grieve are blessed, Harry," she said. "You're among the elect."

Even in the midst of this fresh attack of grief, Harry was flattered to receive the attention of two women at once. He managed to smile and say, "Yes, I should know these things, shouldn't I? I should stop being such a ninny." A chill went through him. "My gosh, that's just what mother said the day we brought her home from the hospital."

"Yes," Sandra replied. "And she wasn't a ninny, and neither are you. You've got to let her give you some more of her strength, Harry. That's what she's there for."

Back at home that evening, Harry finally worked up the courage to read his mother's farewell letter to him. He held the envelope, which was addressed "Harry," in his hands for a long time before slitting it open and removing three sheets of writing paper. He paused a moment longer before he unfolded the sheets and read his mother's familiar flowery handwriting:

My dearest Harry,

My own dear son,

Harry, from the moment I had you, I recognized a special bond between us such as there seldom is between mothers and sons, or even between two human beings. Even though I was an extravagant bohemian artist and you were a shy, obedient little thing destined for a life of scholarship, there was a connection between us that only two kindred souls can know. Our kinship lay in the fact that we never lost our ability to love—or, rather, that we never wandered very far from the source of love. That source is God, of course, and while some people who have had near-death experiences describe God as a white light, I think of Him as a raging fire, something primal, elemental, full of warmth and the churning chaos out of which this world came into being. And love, which comes from God, is like that, as well.

You and I, Harry, somehow were granted a mystical awareness of that fire of love, and we could never be happy unless we were right next to its searing heat. As a result, we were consumed by it, and filled with the desire to bring others to that fire, as well.

What this means (I'm abandoning metaphors now to use practical language, and that is so dreary and boring, don't you think?) is that we went through life determined to share this love with others. That meant being simple and good and forgiving, and not letting other people or things tempt us away from the true path. And that, as you well know, has meant an untold amount of suffering for both of us.

At the end of my life, God brought you back to me that I might die in peace, that I might feel, in this cold world, some of the warmth of His heavenly fire. And He also sent Sandra to you, that you might be warmed and comforted also. But my darling, I'm afraid that people have wandered so far away from the fire of God's love that they've grown afraid of it; they're happy being cold and lost and twisted and practical, and the fire of God's love terrifies them, they regard it as an agent of destruction, not renewal. When people say that they fear Hellfire, I think they're really saying that they fear the fire of God's love, which cleanses us of hate and so is terrifying to those who want to hate.

Every mother wants to shield her son from harm, but knows that isn't always possible, and prays that her son will find the strength to endure life's hardships. I don't have to pray about that, because you are an incredibly strong person, much stronger than I am, and that is because you are even closer than I am to the fire of God's love. You and I are not "hard" people—the blows that life rains down upon us hurt us terribly, and we show that hurt on our faces, and people call us weak. But we're not weak; we endure, because what else can we do but endure and keep on loving, as God commanded us to do? If you were cynical or bitter or angry, you would have a shield of so-called "toughness" around you that would make the blows hurt less. But, my darling, I don't _want_ you to develop that protective shield. I want you to go right on being the same loving, feeling, hurting, forgiving, God-filled person that you are. I want you never to move even an inch away from the fire's comforting warmth, and I want you to bring that warmth to others. That is surely what God made you for—to show others what His love can do, and so bring it to them.

I will never leave you, my darling, never stop praying and interceding for you and Sandra, never stop hovering over you to protect you (if that is permitted). Just remember your purpose in life, my son, and never be filled with anything but the fire of God's love.

And be good to Sandra or I'll come back and wring your neck!

Even in Heaven, my darling, I will never forget how you saved me from the hell of despair and pain. God bless you, my darling—being your mother is the proudest accomplishment that any woman could claim—

Love always and forever,
Mother

Harry laid the letter down and walked over to the window. The blue-black darkness above and around the city lights seemed as far-flung as the universe, as impenetrable as the vital spark. It cried out to be illuminated, not with man-made electricity, but with the consuming fire from which life sprang. The world was in great need of fire-bearers. Whether those bearers' fearful commission was a blessing or a curse, Harry could not say.

CHAPTER THIRTY-NINE

Somehow, the next two and a half weeks passed quickly. Nothing out of the ordinary happened until the Friday before Labor Day, when Frank knocked on the open door of Harry's office and said, "Harry, I need to talk to you."

"Sure, Frank, come on in."

Frank did so and sat down. For the first time in Harry's memory, Frank looked neither enraged nor ebullient but simply depressed. "What's wrong?" Harry asked.

Frank sighed. "I went back to my mama's church the other day—you know, the one that turned heathen and threw me out—and you know what happened?"

"What?"

"I was listening to that fool they've got for a preacher, and he was talking about serving the right master. You know, 'no man can serve two masters'. Well, I was starting to have a feeling that—well, maybe I was serving the *wrong* master."

"What do you mean?"

"I mean, maybe what you were saying about going about life the wrong way—that it was wrong to treat people the way I did—maybe you were right. Maybe I should give up my mama's way of doing things. But I don't want to do that, because my mama was so strong, and her strength protected her from the world. I don't want to be weak like most people. She got awful mad at me when I acted weak. Even though she's dead now, I'm still scared of her. I'm scared she'll come back from the dead and pound my ass into the ground. I don't know if I can stand to go against her. Even if I do and she leaves me alone, the world's gonna cut my throat before nightfall. And I don't want that to happen to me. I've seen it happen to too many other people. I don't want to die."

Harry couldn't think of what to say. At last he came up with, "Are you so certain that you'll be crushed, that something awful will happen to you, Frank?"

"Hell, yes! I know it."

"Well…maybe your life will get better."

"Oh no, it won't. You don't know about these things, Harry. I do."

"So, what are you going to do?"

"I don't know. I'm scared, man. I'm really scared. I never thought of questioning my mama's teachings, I never thought of doubting that hers was the true way to God, until right now. And I probably wouldn't have thought of doing that if it hadn't been for the things you said."

"What things?"

"Well, just what you said about this being the wrong way to go about things. And more than that—you actually seemed as if you believed all that shit. That just—that just plants a seed in your head and gets you thinking, you know? And then what that heathen preacher said about serving the wrong master—it got me thinking that you can serve the right master in the wrong way, know what I mean?"

"Yes," Harry said. "That's about the saddest thing that anyone can do."

"Now, I ain't saying that I was wrong and should change my ways—and I'll never say that my mama was wrong, 'cause I value my life—but I will say that I've started having second thoughts about it. Shit, I've been having second thoughts about my whole damned life. I'm not even sure that this thing between my eyes is my nose anymore. But you know, the devil can cite Scripture for his purpose, and I'm scared that maybe you and that fool preacher and all the rest who say that I'm doing wrong are being used by the devil to tempt me from the true path. No offense, but the devil can use people for his purposes without their knowing it. And for my sake and yours, I got to find out if that's what's happening. But I don't know how."

Harry spread his hands in a helpless gesture. "Frank, I don't think the devil's using me, but there's no way I can possibly prove that to you."

"Yeah, I know," Frank muttered. "I got to find it out for myself. Shit, I got my work cut out for me." He rose from his seat with difficulty, or reluctance, looked at Harry with haunted eyes, and said, "I just wanted you to know that I was having second thoughts, and that it was because of you."

"I'm very glad you did, Frank," said Harry, deeply moved. He rose from his chair and extended a hand to Frank, who, after a pause, took it. "I'll see you on Tuesday."

"Yeah, Tuesday's going to be a big day," Frank muttered. "We're finally going to get rid of that bitch."

"It looks that way. Are you doing anything for the Labor Day weekend?"

"Naw, I'm just going to hang around and pray and think things over. I got a lot to think about."

"You certainly do. I'll be seeing you, Frank."

"Yeah, you too." He turned and left the office.

Harry felt a great dawning sense of triumph. He couldn't save Frank—he couldn't take the credit if Frank turned his life around—but he himself had believed something, and had lived that belief, and that had made a difference to another human being.

His gaze fell upon his mother's picture. He picked it up and looked at her face, and remembered the words of her letter, and the great commission that she had given him—that she had bred in his bones, really. And he knew that he had carried it out.

He kissed his mother's image. "Thank you," he said.

CHAPTER FORTY

The last full day of Harry's and Sandra's lives was a holiday, and they spent most of it lying in bed, not always making love (though they did their share of that), but planning for the future as well. They discussed Cousin Frank's offer to Harry to join his new business, and what accepting it would entail. They would have to move to New York, or rather someplace within commuting distance of it—Long Island, perhaps. Sandra could take an early retirement and still get her government pension; that and Harry's earnings from his new job ("Within a few years, God will be borrowing money from you, dude!" Cousin Frank had said) would enable them to live in comfort. They discussed what portion of this money they could set aside for investments, what portion for savings, what portion for a new house and car, and so forth.

"Isn't it exciting?" Sandra asked after lunch, as they lay snuggled up listening to Rush Limbaugh on the radio. "A whole new, exciting, successful life."

"Yes," Harry replied. "It seems too good to be true."

"It's what you deserve, sweetie. You earned it." She kissed him tenderly. "And you won't have to deal with those jerks anymore."

He sighed. "Sandra, you won't mind if I keep in touch with some of them, will you?"

"Harry, you're a grownup. You don't need to ask my permission to do anything. I'm just so mad at them for the way they treated you. But no, I really want you to do the right thing and be nice to them. Your mother told me that she thought you were sent into my life to show me what love really is. That's what she said in her letter to me."

"Is that right?" Harry asked.

"Yes. It was the most beautiful letter anyone's ever written to me." Tears filled her eyes; she lifted his hand to her eyes and wiped her tears away, then licked them off of his hand. "Do you want to see it?"

"Of course, but...I can't see it now. I know it's a very loving and beautiful letter, but reading it will stab me in the heart, and I...I need to wait a while before letting that happen again."

She kissed his cheek. "I understand." Then she reached underneath him. "Roll over." He obeyed, and she straddled him and began to massage his back.

"That feels good," he moaned.

She giggled. "Do you know what I've always wanted to do? Buy some of those scented, edible body oils and just give you the longest, most sensuous massage you can imagine."

"That would be wonderful."

"Why don't I get some tomorrow, and we can try it out?"

"Please do. But you know what I've always wanted to do?"

"What?" she asked flirtatiously.

"I'd like to get some of those body paints, so that we could draw pictures on each other."

She giggled. "That would be great! I'll see if I can find some in the novelty shop." She patted him playfully on his rear end. "You're so young at heart. You're so sweet."

"Look who's talking," Harry quipped.

"Oh, I know. In fact, in the last couple of months, I've gotten even more so. I mean, I've fulfilled my dreams, and I feel so young! I used to be so frightened of growing old alone. Well, I'm not alone, and I think growing old is the most wonderful thing in the world! You know something? Remember how I told you how scared I was when I got cancer?"

"Yes."

"And remember how scared I was that I'd have to go into chemotherapy and lose my hair? Well, this morning when I went to the bathroom, I looked at myself in the mirror, and I thought, 'You still have your hair, and it looks beautiful!' And I looked at my skin and it was so red and flushed with health, not like that awful ashen color that people who undergo chemo get, and I thought, 'I'm alive!' And then I remembered how your mother touched me after she died, and I thought, 'But I don't have to be afraid of dying, either!' And it was—it was just the most powerful epiphany I've ever had in my life. Now you know why I was so passionate this morning."

"Such a wonderful feeling," Harry whispered so quietly that he could not be heard.

"You know what I'm worried about?" Sandra asked. "Mother."

"Your mother? Why?"

"I've come to realize how much she needs me. She always pushed me and said that she wanted me to be a go-getter like her and dad, but, you know, I think she secretly liked having me so close and having to take care of me sometimes."

"Then you don't want to move away?" Harry asked.

"Oh, no. It's the right thing to do, and mom knows that. It will just be very painful for her, and that worries me."

"Well, we'll do everything we can to make it easier for her."

She kissed him. "Oh, Harry McCreedy, how did you get to be so wonderful? There ought to be a law against anyone being so wonderful."

Harry thought it over. "I guess I just do what's right. Is that so rare?"

"So rare that most of the time it doesn't exist, darling."

CHAPTER FORTY-ONE

Harry rose early on the morning of Tuesday, the fifth of September, and readied himself for work with a lightness in his step and mood. Once he started to whistle, but stopped himself for some reason; still, his heart sang with the joy of this great day. After today, it would all be over. The anxiety that had plagued him continuously for the past year had already subsided; he felt a heavy lightness and sense of freedom, like the feeling that comes after making love, or lying down at the end of a tiring day. In the days and weeks to come, this feeling would surely increase. His last months at Port Arthur Shoes—he and Sandra had decided last night that he would leave the job at the end of December—promised to be a merry lark, a happy sojourn in a kingdom that he had liberated from its despot.

He exchanged an erotic kiss with Sandra before leaving the apartment. "I'm set to meet the president at eleven," he said. "Afterward, we're all going to have a big party and go out to lunch—except for Sally, of course."

"I'll be there at eleven," Sandra promised. "And darling—I am so *very* proud of you."

He blushed and kissed her nose. "Thank you for saying that."

He arrived at work at seven-thirty instead of his usual time of a quarter to eight. Everyone wished him luck, even Frank, who was still in a troubled mood. "I haven't decided what to do," he said. "It's gonna take me a long time to figure it out. But I wish you good luck today."

"You, too, Frank," said Harry.

Sally arrived shortly after eight o'clock and immediately locked herself in her office, refusing to speak with anyone. Harry wondered what she was up to; she should fall down on her knees and thank him for liberating her from her hated job. Apparently she had to keep on playacting to the bitter end rather than admit that someone had gotten the better of her. Albert likewise stayed in the background. "This is your big day," he told Harry, "and I love to ruin people's big days, but I'm keeping away from yours, Harry."

"That's very generous of you," Harry replied.

"I'm not being generous. All of you will jump on my ass if I try to stir things up. Besides, you're all acting so smug already that by lunch time, you'll make me sick."

Harry laughed.

Donald Eldridge, the company president, arrived about nine-thirty. He was a tall and pudgy man with white hair and a red face, a man whose small ferret-like blue eyes regarded the world with a ferocious suspicion. On this particular morning he looked, perhaps, slightly more paranoid than usual, and retired to an empty office with scarcely a word to anyone.

One by one, Harry's coworkers filed into the office and spoke with Eldridge, and then, one by one, filed out with the same story to tell: the president had made a few perfunctory remarks about their having done a good job, then dismissed them. That was strange; perhaps dealing with Sally would be so time-consuming that he could not waste time upon anyone else. Then, shortly before eleven, Bernice went up to Harry and announced that it was his turn. Feeling excited and more than a little pleased with himself, Harry walked to Eldridge's temporary office and knocked on the door.

170

CHAPTER FORTY-TWO

Harry closed the office door and walked toward Eldridge, intent upon shaking his hand. Instead, Eldridge regarded him with a cold gleam in his ferret's eyes and, before Harry could reach him, pointed to a chair and said, "Sit down."

Puzzled, Harry stopped and stared. For a moment terror overwhelmed him, making him lose his equilibrium. But he forced himself to stay calm; surely nothing bad could happen now, after all the hard work that he and the others had done. He sat down obediently and looked Eldridge squarely in the eyes, waiting for him to speak.

"Who do you think you are?" Eldridge demanded frostily.

"Uh…beg pardon?" Harry asked. What was going on here?

"What do you and the other people here think you're doing, trying to twist my arm and make me fire someone just because you don't like her?"

He had lost. This terrible fact struck Harry like a blow to the stomach, knocking all the wind out of him. But how could this have happened? He had to find that out before he allowed himself to grieve. "I—don't quite understand, sir," he said in a voice that he kept deliberately toneless. "We were just informing you that she was behaving in an unprofessional and destructive manner."

"And what does that mean?" he asked.

"Why…it's there in the reports, Mr. Eldridge. What else could it mean?"

"Explain to me what you mean by 'unprofessional.'"

"I—what?" Harry asked, speechless in spite of himself.

"What do you mean by 'unprofessional'? Everyone uses that word, but everyone has a different definition of it. How, then, can I fire someone for acting 'unprofessionally' when no one can tell me what it means?"

Harry regained some of his powers of speech. "Well…Sally was behaving in a very bad way, don't you agree?"

"Of course. Why do you think she's never been promoted

higher than general manager? She's always acted horribly. You'll get no argument from me on that. But that's not the point here. The point is, all of you—especially you, you're the ringleader in this sordid affair—are trying to force me to remove somebody from her job. And that's a very serious undertaking. It's not something that you can enter into lightly."

"But, sir," Harry protested, "we weren't trying to force you to do anything. We were just documenting a very serious matter that was interfering with our productivity around here, poisoning the work environment around here, and calling it to your attention. If I said we hoped that you wouldn't get rid of Sally, that would be a lie—"

"You see!" Eldridge cried with a triumphant pettiness. "You see!"

"—but we weren't trying to force you to do anything. We were just calling this serious problem to your attention, as was our right. And our obligation, really."

"My, my, don't we know what's right and proper," Eldridge mocked. "But calling it to my attention is one thing. This—" he gestured toward the pile of reports on his desk, the reports that Harry and his coworkers had suffered for and labored over for months "—is something else altogether. Just sending me a letter outlining the situation and giving several of the more egregious examples of Sally's behavior would have been perfectly fine. But this huge mountain of reports? That's blatant intimidation. That's strong-arm tactics. That tells me that I don't have any options besides firing Sally. And I'm not going to tolerate it."

Control? Was that what this was all about? This man was going to hurt the future of his own company over a petty question of control?

"You and your coworkers took the matter out of my hands. I decide who gets to stay and who gets to leave around here. Sometimes, of course, action must be taken, but it's up to me to decide when and what kind of action. If that power to make decisions is taken away from me, if someone tries to usurp that power, then nothing will work and everything suffers. Do you understand?"

Harry did not want to understand, and did not have the strength to talk. He was sucked down into a black mire of despair.

"You know, I've been looking for an excuse to get rid of that black bitch," Eldridge continued. "If you'd just sent me a letter about this problem, then I could have had that opportunity. I could have gotten rid of her, and you might just have gotten yourself a promotion. But no, you couldn't trust me. You had to try and twist my arm. You blew it, Harry. You're totally screwed, and so am I, and so are your coworkers. You'll never get rid of Sally now."

"What?" Harry asked, his voice a cross between a gasp and a cry of protest.

"Sally's staying. And let me tell you, your life around here is not going to be pleasant."

"But she hates it here...she already has a job lined up with her father..."

"I know all that. But she told me last night that she's decided to stay. She doesn't like to be manipulated, either."

Harry reached the bottom of his pit of despair. *We're doomed,* he thought. There would be no holding Sally back now.

"Several of your coworkers mentioned that you were planning on leaving here soon," Eldridge asked. "Is that true?"

"Yes," Harry whispered sadly. "At the end of the year."

"Say you'll leave a month from today and you can stay on until then. Otherwise, your ass is going out the door right now."

At least I can leave of my own free will, Harry thought sadly. *At least I still have a little control over my own life left.* This thickheaded egotist was right: it was all about power and control.

"I'll leave in a month," he whispered.

"Good. Then you can stay, and none of this will go on your record. I just hope that you have the balls to deal with Sally, because it is *not* going to be pretty around here, my friend. If you'd just helped me out, and then let me deal with it, then maybe you could have been sitting in her place right now. But no, you had to have delusions of power, of taking my right to make the decisions around here away from me. You've made your own pig sty, and it's full of shit, and you're going to have to wallow in it, and I don't care if you drown. Now get out of my office."

These final words of malediction did not hurt; Harry was too overcome with grief to feel anything. Perhaps he would never be able to feel anything again; perhaps it was better that way.

"What did I say?" Eldridge cried. "Get out of my office!"

As quickly as his broken spirit would allow, Harry got to his feet and, like a tired, crippled old man, shuffled out the door.

CHAPTER FORTY-THREE

Sandra was waiting for him in the hallway. As soon as she caught sight of him, a look of fear came over her face. "What happened?" she asked.

Harry didn't know what to say. The only possible response was to open his mouth and let out a long, loud, mad laugh. But for now he was too overcome to find the humor in this insanity.

Sandra hurried over to him and held him at arm's length. "Harry, what *happened?*" she cried.

"He said—" Harry began, lost his voice, and then started over. "He said that he wasn't going to do anything about our complaints because—we tried to take the matter out of his hands."

Sandra went pale, and her mouth became a widening O of shock. "What?" she gasped.

"He said we were trying to take the matter out of his hands and force him to take action. He doesn't like that, so he says he...can't do anything about it."

Sandra put a hand to her mouth. "Oh, no!" she said. "Oh, my God!"

Harry sighed. "He said he'd been wanting to get rid of Sally for a long time, but that he couldn't do anything now because we tried to...usurp his authority, I guess."

She held him to her. "Oh, my poor baby," she said. "Oh, my poor baby. They can't do this to you, my poor baby."

Harry sagged in her arms and leaned his head on her shoulder. "I worked so hard," he said, "and now it's all come to nothing."

"I know, I know. My poor baby. They have no right to do this to you, my poor baby." She kissed his cheeks, then his mouth, frantically, again and again. "Oh, my poor baby."

"I tried so hard—" he said in a deathly whisper.

She pulled back from him. "Harry, you've got to get out of here now."

"He said if I agreed to leave in a month, he wouldn't fire

me. So I agreed."

"Harry, *quit!* You can't stay in this filthy place another minute."

"But…what about the others? Sally will make their lives a living hell."

"Forget about them! They're not worth it. They're so far beneath you…they're lower than the dust on your shoes. Everyone is around here. You've got to get out of here."

He sighed again. "Perhaps you're right. But I can't think right now. I feel like someone just drove a Mac truck through the center of me."

"I know, my poor darling, let's go home."

"No," he said, "I've—got to talk to the others."

"All right, but then we're going home."

The sound of a door opening made them turn round, and they saw Eldridge step into the hallway.

Sandra's face twisted with rage, and her eyes flashed fury. "How could you!" she cried at Eldridge. "After all he did to help this filthy, rotten place. How could you!"

Eldridge lowered his head in embarrassment and, for an instant, did not know what to do.

"How could you!" she said. "What kind of a man are you, you—you rotten bastard!"

Harry laid a hand on her shoulder. "Sandra, honey—"

"Answer me!" Sandra cried as Eldridge turned and walked away as fast as he could without running. "Answer me, you coward!"

"Sandra!" Harry yelled, and the sharpness in his voice quieted her. She looked at him, and grief quenched her fury. "I'm sorry, darling," she said, "but I—I can't believe what he did. I couldn't let him get away with it."

He kissed her forehead. "Come on," he said, and led her to the break room.

They stepped into the break room, then recoiled in horror. Sally was sitting there, regarding Harry with a distant, ageless look of triumph. "Ooooh, you're all upset," she said softly. "You got to get your wife to fight your battles for you. I always knew you was pussy-whipped."

Harry managed to say, "Go away, Sally. No one's interested in talking to you."

"Oh, they aren't, are they? Well, they're going to listen to me anyway."

"Let's go," he whispered to Sandra, and they turned and left.

"Come back here!" Sally screamed. "You get both your asses back here NOW!"

Harry, amazed at his own composure, whispered to Sandra, "Keep walking, and don't look back," and led her through the door leading to the main show room.

"GODDAMNIT, I SAID GET BACK HERE NOW!" Sally shrieked. Everyone on the showroom floor—all of Harry's coworkers, as well as the five customers in the store (two men, two women, and a young child), stopped and stared.

"MOTHERFUCKERS!" Sally's voice, which was rapidly approaching, boomed. "DON'T YOU TURN YOUR BACKS ON ME, YOU HEAR? I AIN'T SOME NIGGER YOU CAN TURN YOUR BACKS ON!"

The door burst open, and Sally charged through it. Harry and Sandra, who had advanced several paces into the show room, stopped and began to look back. Before either could turn round fully, Sally smashed her fist into Harry's jaw.

Harry was tall and strong, so the blow did not knock him down, but its force made him stagger. Something thick and wet and repulsive coursed through his mouth, then spilled down his chin onto both the floor and his expensive suit: blood. For an instant there was a stunned silence; then Sally shot her foot forward and kicked him in the groin. This blow was strong enough to bring Harry down, and he fell to his knees, then onto his face.

Sandra let out a primal growl of fury and sprang upon Sally, almost knocking her down. *"Leave him alone!"* she cried, and tried to jam her fingers into Sally's eyes.

"OH, SO YOU WANT TO FIGHT ME, DO YOU?" Sally said. "YOU WANT TO FUCK WITH ME?" She drew back her fist and, in the same instant, drove it into Sandra's nose, flattening that beautiful and well-proportioned piece of architecture, sending gouts of blood spurting from it.

All of the coworkers were running up by now. Bernice caught Sandra as she staggered backward. The others piled upon Sally, holding her arms and squirming body.

"YOU WANT TO FUCK WITH ME?" Sally cried at the dazed, bleeding Sandra. "YOU THINK YOU CAN FUCK WITH ME? YOU THINK YOU SO BIG AND IMPORTANT AND WHITE? WELL, HONEY, MY DADDY COULD SELL BOTH YOU SORRY WHITE ASSES INTO SLAVERY AND HAVE YOUR WHOLE FAMILIES KILLED! WHAT YOU THINK OF THAT? HUH? WHAT YOU THINK OF THAT?"

"Sally, *shut up!*" Richard yelled, getting her in a chokehold. She squirmed and wriggled and kicked furiously, connecting with shins and legs and arms, but still everyone held on. She struggled for a moment more, then abruptly went limp.

Richard loosened his chokehold, and the others let Sally go. Exhausted, gasping for breath, Richard began to lower Sally's limp body to the floor.

In an instant she was up and free. "HAH!" she cried. "I FOOLED YOU!" With the grace and skill of a ballerina she dodged out of everyone's reach, grabbed a thick wooden chair that sat nearby, pirouetted over to Harry, and broke the chair over his head.

Forgetting her own pain and dazed condition, Sandra sprang forward and clamped her hands around Sally's throat.

"I TOLD YOU NOT TO FUCK WITH ME!" Sally said. She reached out and grabbed one of Sandra's breasts, then yanked hard.

Sandra screamed and let go of Sally's throat. Sally grabbed Sandra's throat in turn and rushed her forward, ramming her up against a row of shelves. Then the row of shelves leaned over too far, lost its balance, and crashed to the floor, with Sandra atop it.

"AND THAT'S WHAT HAPPENS WHEN YOU FUCK WITH ME!" Sally cried, then delivered a series of hard and vicious kicks to Sandra's head. The side of her head caved in, and blood began to flow freely and copiously from her wound, as if its natural function was to spill onto the ground, not to course through her veins.

All of her underlings, joined now by the two male customers, piled onto Sally in an instant. "FUCK IT, LET ME GO!" she cried, but could not break free. "FUCK YOU, LET ME GO! DON'T YOU KNOW WHO YOU FUCKING WITH? YOU THOUGHT YOU COULD OUTSMART ME, BUT I FUCKED YOU UP INSTEAD! I *WIN!*"

Richard balled up his fist and punched Sally in her kidneys. She let out a whoop of surprise as all of the air and strength left her body. Then Frank socked her in the face once, twice, three times, knocking her down. Still he kept hitting her, then grabbed her head and began to bang it against the floor, grunting all the while with rage and hatred. Then they pulled Frank away, and he collapsed, sobbing and gasping, to the floor.

Richard picked up Sally in his thick arms and carried her out of the show room, all the while yelling for someone to "Call an ambulance!" and "Call the police!" Denise, her face a mask of shock and grief, ran to do so.

Meanwhile, one of the customers was kneeling over Sandra. "She's dead," he announced.

Bernice clutched her face and wailed, "Oh God, no, oh God no no no no no no no no…" One of the women customers put her arms around her and led her away.

The customer turned his attention to Harry. "He's still alive," he said, "but he needs to be gotten to a hospital fast."

"It's…it's on its way," Albert replied. For once, his voice was soft, childlike, and frightened. He surveyed the carnage dully, as if it were the letters of some alien tongue.

"There must be a policeman outside," the man said. "I'll see if I can flag one down." He hurried outside, where the second female customer and her young child had already fled in terror.

Frank, who had stopped weeping, got to his feet. "I'll sit with Harry," he mumbled to no one in particular. "I got something to say to him. I'll take care of him."

He went over and knelt down beside him. Harry's face was

marred by an ugly purple bruise and by the dark blood that poured from the gash on his forehead. It was pitiful, Frank thought, that it should all end this way. He bent over the unconscious figure and began to speak.

CHAPTER FORTY-FOUR

For a few moments, Harry had been totally unconscious, unable even to dream; then he climbed slowly back toward awareness, but his weakened condition, and the terrible pain in his head, kept him from opening his eyes or speaking. Even if he had had the strength to speak, his mouth was filled with a foul-tasting, sticky substance—blood, probably—and it would take even longer for him to work up the strength to spit it out.

A voice that, after an instant, he recognized as Frank's came from somewhere just above his head. "You lied to me," Frank said with quiet bitterness. "You said that I'd be free, that things would be better, that I wouldn't have to put up with shit no more. You said that I could stop fighting, that I didn't need to fight, that I could lay down my arms and still be safe. Well, I gave it a try, and where am I? That bitch is still shitting on all of us, and she's really shitted on you now, ain't she? Last Sunday, you know what I did? I decided to stop going to my old church. I decided to find a church that preached that pissy-assed false Gospel of peace and love that you white folks use to keep us down. I promised God I'd try to live that way for a while. And now what's happened? Everything's over. I've laid down my arms, and now I'm gonna get killed. This sinful world's gonna run right over me, just like my mama said it would. My mama—" there was a terrified, grieving catch in his voice "—my mama is going to kill me. She's going to hunt me down and *kill* me. That is, if this world don't kill me first. And if the world gets to me first, then she's going to meet me at the gates of Heaven and cast me down to Hell, just like Michael did to Satan when the angels rebelled against God."

Poor Frank, Harry thought, so corrupted by a hate-filled, counterfeit Gospel and by hate-filled, counterfeit people. He would have to reassure him once he had the strength to open his eyes and speak. He felt that strength slowly returning now. In just a moment, he could make the effort to do those vital things.

Frank's voice rose to an agonized wail. "I'm going to die

and go to Hell, and it's all your fault!"

Then there were louder sounds that, while they came from farther away, might have been yelled directly into his ear: the sounds of more than one woman screaming in terror. For an instant, one of the screams composed itself into words: "FRANK, *NO!*"

A sudden pain—the pain only a boxcutter can cause—ripped across and into his throat. It was hard to tell which element of the pain was worse—its depth, its breadth, or its rapidity. But there was no time to dwell on that; in an instant all of the strength that enabled his eyes to see, his tongue to form words, or his heart to beat suddenly shot out of him. Where was it going? Somewhere outside of himself, where its life giving powers would be wasted. He must go and bring it back.

He left his body, and suddenly found himself in a different sphere of existence, where he could once again move and see and speak. But this place was so vast and featureless; where could he go? Suddenly his mother and Sandra were at his side, and while they looked the same as they always had, they looked somehow purer, as if their hidden essence had flamed forth and transfigured them. They embraced and kissed him, and the love that their touch communicated was more powerful than any he had ever known. Their eyes shone with a light much smaller, but infinitely purer, than the sun's.

Sandra and his mother tugged at him gently as if to say, *We'll show you the way.* He turned round and saw all of the chaos and bloody rage of the world he had left behind. There was so much more to be done. But it was late, yet early, in the eternal day, and Sandra and his mother had somewhere they wanted to take him.

ABOUT THE AUTHOR

JAMES JEFFREY PAUL was born in 1963 and grew up in Orlando, Florida. He graduated with honors and distinction from Duke University and earned master's degrees from the University of Florida in Gainesville and the University of North Carolina in Chapel Hill. *Harry McCreedy* is his first published book. He is currently working on writing projects in various media. James Jeffrey Paul welcomes comments from readers and critics. He can be reached in care of his publisher or at the following e-mail address: j.j.paul@worldnet.att.net.